R

BEST SELLER ROMANCE

A chance to read and collect some of the best-loved novels from Mills & Boon—the world's largest publisher of romantic fiction.

Every month, four titles by favourite Mills & Boon authors will be re-published in the *Best Seller Romance* series.

A list of other titles in the *Best Seller Romance* series can be found at the end of this book.

Violet Winspear

DESIRE HAS NO MERCY

MILLS & BOON LIMITED
15–16 BROOK'S MEWS
LONDON W1A 1DR

First published in Great Britain 1979
by Mills & Boon Limited

Reprinted 1979
This edition 1985

ISBN 0 263 75017 5

Set in Linotype Plantin 10 on 11½ pt.
02–0185

Made and printed in Great Britain by
Richard Clay (The Chaucer Press) Ltd,
Bungay, Suffolk

CHAPTER ONE

JULIA fled from the wedding reception, desperate to be alone for a few minutes so she could recover her shattered composure.

Her hand clenched the stonework of the balcony where she stood and she felt shaken to the core. How dared Rome Demario come here, strolling among the guests with a champagne cocktail held in his hand, looking so boundlessly sure of himself in a beige suit of Italian cut, his darkness intensified by a speckless white shirt. She had wildly hoped never to see him again and it had come as a deep, primitive shock when he had walked in so boldly on her sister's wedding reception.

She half-closed her eyes and a tremor ran all the way through her ... oh God, she had tried so hard to forget his Latin face, the firm yet full lips, the lean jaw and bronzed neck joining the well-carried shoulders. And most of all she had tried not to remember those smoke-grey eyes lit from within so that in anger and passion they were incandescent.

God help her, she had burned in those eyes that indelible night in Naples. His gaze had felt as if it were touching her when she walked ahead of him up the scarlet-carpeted stairs that led to his private domain above the casino. His eyes had dwelt on her with such deliberation when he had closed the door and there was sudden silence after the noisy hum of the gaming rooms.

The memory of that night swept over Julia in a wave and she took deep breaths of air in order to steady her swimming senses. She had prayed never to see again the man who had so disrupted her life, so that now Verna was safely married she had to make plans for her own future. An uncertain and rather frightening future for which Rome Demario was directly to blame.

'I won't go down on my knees like a beggar,' she had said to him. 'I'll see you in hell first.'

'It may well be in heaven,' he told her. 'One can be so confused with the other, that's why sinners enjoy more heaven than the saints.'

'Enjoy your sin, Signor Demario,' she said. 'You'll live to regret it, if there's any justice.'

Justice! Julia could have laughed aloud had there been a vestige of humour in her heart, which there wasn't. She couldn't even have wept, for it all struck deeper than tears could have eased.

It had started years ago, long before she was forced to pay off Verna's gambling debts in such a pride-shattering way. It had started when Rome Demario's widowed mother used to come to the Van Holden house on Grand Drive to assist with the housework, a dark-haired, slender woman whose grey eyes always looked sad, and whose young son was often seen by Julia running errands for her haughty grandmother.

One afternoon there had been a birthday party for Verna, with lots of ice-cream and cake, and smartly dressed children dancing to a record-player in one of the large ground-floor rooms. When Julia noticed the Demario boy watching the fun through the French windows she had thought it would be a nice gesture to offer him a strawberry ice-cream, which instead of eating he had deliberately dropped on to her new shoes with the little shining buckles. Like a little idiot she had burst into tears and Grandma Van Holden had angrily told the boy's mother not to come and work at the house any more. Mrs Demario had gone very white and had pleaded that work was hard to find and she had a growing boy to feed. Grandma had turned a deaf ear to her pleading and had marched Julia back to the party, telling her in a voice that carried that in future she was to stay well away from bad-mannered Italian boys.

As long ago as their childhood had been lit in Rome Demario a flame of hurt pride and anger, which finally in Naples he had quenched by humbling her pride.

The single blessing was that he hadn't made her cry, as she had cried when the ice-cream splashed her buckled shoes. When she left the casino she had walked out unbowed, the IOUs in her purse. At the hotel she had given them to Verna and warned her that such reckless gambling in the future might cost her the man she was soon to marry, a socially prominent and ambitious young lawyer. Verna wanted to be his wife and she had gratefully promised Julia that never again would she even look at a roulette wheel.

'But how did you persuade the owner of the casino to let you have the slips?' Verna looked curiously at Julia, but fortunately the obvious answer didn't occur to her. She had forgotten the Demario boy and seemed unaware that when they were children his mother had worked for their grandmother. 'It's such a lot of money, Julia, and he looked so—ruthless.'

'I expect he was feeling in the mood to be—generous.' Julia said it ironically. 'I told him you were getting married and he said to call the IOUs his wedding gift.'

Those had been his parting words to her. 'Call these an Italian's wedding gift to your sister. Let's hope she's luckier in love.'

A shadowed look crossed Julia's face, and then her spine stiffened as she caught the aroma of a cigar . . . a long thin

Italian cigar such as the one Rome Demario had been enjoying at the casino that night, its fragrant smoke drifting about his dark head as he gazed across the room at her, compellingly grey-eyed, supple and tall, and more ruthless than Verna would ever know.

Julia had backed away from him with all the instinctive fear of a girl whose reserve and natural dignity were suddenly aware of forces beyond her control; a Van Holden whose destiny had been so well protected until the demise of Grandma Van Holden and the discovery that for years she'd been living on her dwindling capital until there was very little left for her granddaughters to subsist on. She had arrogantly denied them any sort of business training so it hadn't been easy for either of them to find employment. A friend of the family had taken on Verna as a social companion and that was how the sisters came to be taking a holiday in Italy. The kindly woman had insisted that Julia join them, and right away she and Julia had discovered a mutual joy in Italian opera, which Verna found less entertaining.

It was those evenings at the opera which had led to Verna seeking a diversion more to her liking ... there had been other times when she had gambled, but never before had she got herself so deeply in debt. It wasn't until Julia came face to face with the owner of the casino that she realised why the debt had been allowed to mount up in such an alarming way. The moment she saw him Julia knew him and was aware that he still hated the Van Holdens.

'You've grown up to be quite the lady, haven't you, Miss Julia?' His eyes had mocked her as they travelled up and down her slim figure. 'Are you still generous with the strawberry ice-cream?'

A riot of emotions seethed in Julia as each vivid memory slid through her mind like pictures on a screen. She was gripping the balcony stonework so hard that she could feel her fingernails breaking, for he was there behind her, silently watching her and remembering as she was the details of their last encounter, etched with a clarity the weeks in between had failed to erase.

Julia felt so tormented she could hardly bear it, that he should know her with such intimacy when everyone else was so certain of her poised coolness, her dedication to her work at the art gallery, her saving of herself and her feelings for 'the right man' as her friends fondly and amusedly called him ... Paul Wineman, the distinguished art critic who had begun to pay her some courtly attention.

'*Buon giorno, signorina.*' The cigar smoke drifted closer and Julia tensed as her nerves felt a silent and supple approach, the tread of a tiger, darkly tanned from his head to his heels ... a pagan who enjoyed the Italian sun on the high terrace of his casino, so he had carelessly told her when he held her and contrasted her skin with his own. 'Milk and honey,' he had breathed. 'They mix well, don't they?'

'Go away!' Julia had wanted to sound cold and angry, but her voice betrayed the pain and fear of a girl in trouble. 'You have no right to be here, Signor Demario. You weren't invited.'

'But I was, Signorina Van Holden. Your sister sent me an invitation.'

'Verna did what?' Julia swung round and was quite unable to suppress a gasp when she saw him standing only a few inches away from her, with not a crease in the fine suiting that covered his lean hard body. A pain stabbed deep inside her and she felt an intense awareness of the link she must soon find the courage to have cut, so she'd be free of him. Free to try and live the gracious, ordered life he had so disturbed with his vengeful arrogance.

'To thank me,' he drawled, 'for returning the IOUs her

fiancé wouldn't have liked receiving.'

Julia swayed against the stone parapet and at once he was beside her, the rim of a champagne glass at her lips. 'Don't faint—sip a little of this.'

Julia didn't dare to faint. A couple of guests at the wedding were in the medical profession and she had sworn to herself that no one was going to know that she, who prided herself on being poised and coolly detached from the romantic blunders of other girls, had been forced into a situation which could scandalise the family her sister had married into only an hour ago.

She shivered and swallowed the champagne with an effort. It revived her so she could feel Rome Demario's hand pressing against her body, reminding her acutely of that other time when she had been without defence in his arms.

'You had no right to come here!' she said tensely. 'So you could gloat a-and look at me in front of my friends as if you—you——'

'As if I own part of you?' he murmured, and his grey eyes looked directly down into hers, making her burn with a sudden overwhelming blush ... it seemed to go all over her and she gasped at what she saw in his eyes, a rekindling of those memories of a night when for a brief moment it had seemed as if he might give her those IOUs without demanding that she pay for them. He had stood there, his shoulders against the door, and he had gestured around the beautifully furnished room as if to remind her that no longer was he the errand boy at her grandmother's house.

'We are now man and woman,' he said to her. 'Now we are equal.'

'I don't consider myself the equal of a gambler who allows young girls to play for high stakes at his tables,' she had retorted freezingly. 'I wouldn't want to be that low.'

'So I am low, eh?' It was then he had approached her with such deliberate intent. 'Then I shall bring you down to my level, my high and mighty Miss Van Holden.'

Julia shrank against the stonework of the hotel balcony and her face was so white that her eyes seemed to throw green shadows on to her skin.

'You will not look like that!' he exclaimed. 'I didn't come to this wedding to gloat over you. As a matter of fact I was going to tear up the invitation, and then I thought to myself how intriguing it was that Rome Demario should receive an invitation to a Van Holden reception. I recall a time when he wasn't good enough to mingle with their refined guests.'

'That's what this—this torture is all about, isn't it?' Julia's eyes blazed into his. 'You're getting your own back, making one of the Van Holdens pay for something that happened a long time ago. I couldn't help it that my grandmother behaved so arrogantly and dismissed your mother from her employment. I didn't want your mother to be out of work. I was only a child and you made me cry—something you'll never do again, Signor Demario. Never!'

He stared down at Julia's face, utterly white except for the smudges of shadow beneath her green eyes. Her face had a slender delicacy, a quiver she couldn't control to the full soft lips that betrayed a passion her cool look of poise was inclined to deny. Most people would have said at once that Verna Van Holden was more ardent than her sister, but the truth simply was that she was less innately shy and sensitive, and could never have suffered as Julia was suffering right now.

The very touch of Rome Demario was insufferable to Julia. When he looked at her it was as if he stripped her of clothing, of virtue, of every decency she had held dear not out of prudery but because she was so innately modest, with reserves of a deep loving kind he had forced, made her yield; a throbbing, sensual destruction of the chastity which had been hers to give with love ... which he had taken without love.

'When I look at you,' she said, 'I feel cheap and dirty. I'd want to die if my friends—least of all my sister—knew why you really came here. I couldn't bear for them to know!'

'Something,' he said very quietly, 'is very much amiss. You will tell me—come, I insist on knowing!' His arm gripped her and he moved in closer until his long legs were pressing against her and she could feel the masculine warmth of his body penetrating through the soft material of her dress; leaf-green chiffon silk, clinging softly to the slim soft contours of her body. Closer, his warm hardness a threatening reminder of what he had done to her and what his physical dominance was capable of doing again.

'You're an affront,' she gasped. 'Did you imagine—what did you think, *signore*, that I'd be thrilled to see you? Do you fondly imagine you've aroused pangs of burning hunger in me and I'm thrilled to see your face again? It's a face I've hoped never to see again!' Her eyes were fixed wide and tormented on the Italian features she had tried so hard to blot from her mind ... a look Bernini had surely visualised when he painted the canvas she had seen in the Borghese art gallery in Rome, leaning over the seduced Proserpina.

'I've aroused something, *signorina*.' That intent look was there in his eyes and Julia was trapped by his lean body whose strength she had tried to fight, learning the hard way how much deep-coiled power there was in the shoulders and arms of Rome Demario. He had subdued her then, and he'd do it again if he had to ... Julia saw the threats in the depths of his eyes where those devil fires burned ...

those fires which had still smouldered behind his dark lashes when the dawn light came through the windows high above a Neapolitan street and she was allowed to leave him, feeling as if shame was something she would never cease to live with. She remembered now that he had murmured *arrivederci*.

'You have about you a look I don't quite remember.' Suddenly he had his fingers beneath her chin and was forcing up her face so he could study its every angle. He moved his long fingers up against her cheek and touched a fingertip to her shadowed eyes.

'Let me go before someone sees us!' She was arching away from him, trying somehow to escape the touch of his body ... her own body was reacting to him, as if it were separated from her mind and was primitively drawn to his as if in some strange effort to protect what she intended to kill.

'I beg of you, *signore*! My sister's in-laws would be affronted if any of them saw me like this—with you——'

'With me?' he mockingly echoed. 'The Italian whose mother used to peel potatoes in your grandmother's kitchen? What is he now, eh? He's very much Italian and he's putting one and one together and it's adding up to three. You're with child, aren't you?'

'No!' It was almost a scream, which he swiftly stifled with his hand.

'You are having a baby,' he said quietly, 'and I am the father. I feel it, Julia, so don't attempt to deny it. Your face is more slender but your body is less so—you are carrying my child!'

'No,' she said again, desperate to convince him that it wasn't true. 'Babies don't come from that sort of thing—from a woman's hatred of the man who—who forces her to sleep with him. You're the very last man whose child I'd want to be carrying!'

'All the same, my child is here.' His hand had slid down and was now in contact with her stomach, his touch drivingly warm through the fine material of her dress, whose soft folds concealed that slight burgeoning of her figure ... unless a hand touched her as Rome Demario's was touching her.

'How dare you?' she breathed. 'Your arrogance and sensuality are enough to make me ill!'

'Enough to make you pregnant, *carina*.' That strange kindling was there in his eyes, making them more intensely beautiful that such a man's eyes had the right to be. Julia writhed in an effort to get away from him, her hand reaching up convulsively as if to claw his eyes from his head. He flung aside the champagne glass as he gripped her wrist and it fell with a splintering crash to the pavement of the balcony, some of the wine splashing her silk-clad ankle, reminding her with acuteness of another time when he had flung ice-cream over her shoes ... the bitter roots of all this had sprung from that moment.

'Tell me,' he insisted, his lips against her ear. 'The baby is mine, isn't it? We were together in Naples about seven weeks ago and you look and feel like a girl in the early stages of a baby. Come, why deny it when something can be done about it?'

'W-what do you mean?' Her eyes locked with his, blending her green-eyed resentment with the brilliance of his gaze. 'Are you talking about an abortion?'

'A—what?' Something writhed across his face that made instant fear clutch at Julia's heart. His hands tightened until they were hurting her, bringing her so close to him that she could feel the anger seething in his body. 'Do you imagine, my girl, that I would permit such an outrage?'

'Outrage led to this, or have you forgotten, *signore*, in your Italian concern for your embryo?'

'So it is mine?' Astounding as it seemed to Julia he looked curiously pleased and taking hold of her hand he kissed the wrist and then turned it so he could place his lips in her palm.

'Don't!' Julia jerked her hand from the warmth of his mouth. 'It isn't something to look smug about! You should feel thoroughly ashamed of yourself, but I doubt if you know the meaning of the word.'

'Ashamed?' He looked at her in astonishment. 'We have made a child and I shall arrange right away that my son or daughter has my name.'

'You're out of your mind!' Julia gasped. 'I—I don't intend to bear the child——'

'You have some other intention?' His black brows were drawn abruptly together into a dangerous frown, his eyes glittering at their centres with a diamond-shaped brilliance. 'The child is in you, living and growing. Are you trying to tell me that you——' He swallowed, as if the words would choke him. 'You aren't going to kill my child, do you hear me? You are going to have it!'

'Not while I breathe.' Julia's heart was pounding, as it had that night in Naples. 'It's bad enough that I've been put in this predicament by you without being arrogantly told that I'm to go on carrying a baby I don't want. Do you honestly think I'd have a child of yours? Do you fondly imagine I'd be seen by my sister and friends in such a state?'

'I care nothing for your sister or your friends.' He bit the words out with his strong white teeth. 'I only care about what is mine and I shall see to it that you don't put yourself in some smart clinic with the intention of murdering what is part of me. That is your plan, of course, but as my wife you'll have no need to kill the baby or risk your own life in order to pretend to your friends that you are still a virgin.'

Julia was lost for words. She could only gaze at Rome Demario in dumb astonishment, until suddenly she started to laugh and he had to shake her in order to make her stop.

'Your wife?' she exclaimed. 'You think I'd stoop to marrying you? I'd sooner throw myself under a bus!'

'No doubt.' His hands gripped her and his eyes glittered as they held hers. You are welcome to do whatever you fancy, my dear Julia—after my child is born in wedlock, with my name on the birth certificate as the father and yours as the mother. Do you hear me and understand me, Julia? You are going to marry me whether you want it or not.'

'Never,' she said fiercely. 'I hate and despise you for what you've done to my life. You used me to even an old score and I shall never forgive you for assuming that night in Naples that I was as experienced as those other women who run up debts in your casino and pay their bills in your arms. It's a pity I wasn't experienced, then I wouldn't be pregnant with your——'

He stopped the word by pressing a hand over her mouth. 'There is no need for that—no need to let the hatred into the bloodstream of the baby. What has happened has to be put right and there is only one way to do it, and you know it in your heart.'

His hand slid from her mouth and moved almost caressingly to her shoulder, where it lay warm and heavy through the material of her dress. She shivered and remembered the feel of his hand on her skin, the startled exclamation against the hollow of her throat when he found himself making love to a girl who had never been with a man before. His body had tensed as if he tried to pull back, but something—passion, bitter boyhood memories—had overridden the impulse. He had made her give in to him until she was aware of nothing but the darkness and the primitive ritual ... passion and terror blending together until she couldn't tell one from the other.

When daylight came she had wanted only to hurry away and forget ... a forlorn hope as it turned out.

'Don't touch me!' She shrugged her shoulder away from his hand. 'You have no right to me or the child. You forced me to get this way, but you can't force me to go through with it. I can't—I won't! I have a life of my own to live and I won't drag out the next few months getting huge with your Italian brat. I hate it! I hate you! I hate what you've turned me into!'

'You're getting hysterical, so stop it, Julia, unless you want a sound shaking.' His dark face was adamant as he looked at her, the lean jaw set and firm. 'You're welcome to hate me, but all the same you are going to listen to reason and marry me. I am Italian, and that means I am also a Catholic, and I forbid you to even think about terminating the life of our child. Yes, Julia, *our child.* You might not like hearing me say it, but it happens to be true. Whatever led to its conception, the child is a fact of nature, and if I have to stand by you night and day for the next seven months I shall do so in order that you won't harm the infant or yourself. When you are safely over the birth, then I shall get a nursemaid for it and you can leave me. I make you that promise, on my heart, here and now. I neither make threats nor promises that I don't carry out—you know that, don't you?'

Julia gazed back into his eyes, so astoundingly grey and luminous in all that darkness. Darkly tanned skin, thick black hair, lashes like soot that spread shadows on his face. A striking man she might have admired for his looks had they met in different circumstances; she was a person who was sensitive to physical beauty, but he had unforgivably flawed her as a person and she felt she could have put a knife into him.

'I couldn't live with you,' she said distinctly. 'It would make me ill to have to see you night and day for the next seven months. Haven't you got it into your arrogant head, *signore*? I despise everything about you, the look of you, the sound of you, and especially the touch of you. I can hardly bear it that I have inside me something you have put there. I hate the baby! I don't want it and I am perfectly in the right to have it terminated. I shall tell the doctor I was raped.'

He flinched when she said that, and if it were possible went pale under the darkness of his skin. His facial bones seemed to stand out with additional clarity and the pupils of his eyes expanded until their incandescent grey was almost obscured by the dark centres. He looked as if she had kicked him in the throat, for he seemed unable to speak for several long moments.

Julia felt a thrust of pleasure that she had actually bruised his pride. She didn't care that they had actually struck a bargain, her sister's IOUs in exchange for her intimate company for a night. Julia knew he had assumed she was a woman of the world; her background as a Van Holden, her manner, her soignée style of dress and grooming, all these would have led him to such a conclusion. It was now forlornly too late to wonder if his intentions had been really serious when he suggested they go upstairs to his private apartment. She had been frightened but determined not to beg for his charity. Tearing a leaf out of Grandma Van Holden's almanac of arrogant manners she had called him lowdown, and that was when he had laid down his cigar and backed her through the door of his bedroom.

The terror of the moment sprang back into Julia's eyes and with a sudden tearless cry she turned to the balcony parapet and buried her face against the stone.

'Don't do that.' His hands swung her around and pulled her to his shoulder. 'I know how you feel and I want to make amends. Come, stop trembling like that or you'll injure the baby.'

Deep spasmodic tremors that she found impossible to control, his hand moving up and down her spine in an attempt to help her overcome them, her body pressed to his as if he tried to give her some of his strength.

'You're frightened, Julia,' he murmured. 'You know what it means to go to one of those places where they lay you on a table and treat your body with indignity. Believe me, child, I never meant to make you pregnant—it happened—it happened, but we can put it right. I can put it right if you'll let me. I'll stand by you and shield you. You can think of me as a guardian and no more than that. The fact that I am a husband will be no more than a necessary formality. When the child it born you will never need to see it ever again. Julia, are you listening to me?'

Before she could answer, a voice spoke from the long windows leading out to the balcony.

'Julia, my dear, whatever is wrong? Who is this man?'

At the sound of the voice Julia jerked her head away from Rome Demario's shoulder and her eyes met the dark ones of Paul Wineman, standing there looking at her with a great deal of puzzlement, and a hint of anger.

The man referred to, Rome Demario, swung round in his supple way to confront Wineman. 'I am Julia's fiancé,' he said deliberately. 'She and I have decided to be married as soon as possible. Have you any objections?'

Wineman stared at the tall Italian who stood so close to Julia. 'Is this actually true?' he demanded of her. 'Is this fellow really telling me that you've become engaged to marry him?'

No! Julia wanted to cry out the word, to protest that such an idea was ludicrous, that she wanted an ordered, gracious marriage with a man of her own choosing whose interests were similar to her own. But stark in her mind was another image . . . that of a clinical room where a white-gowned figure leaned over her body with a gleaming instrument in his hand. Unaware she clutched at Rome Demario, her fingers digging into him.

'Yes,' she heard herself say, 'I'm going to marry this man.'

'I see.' Paul Wineman slowly took a thin gold cigarette-case from his pocket and opened it. As he tapped a cigarette against the gold his eyes flicked from Julia to Rome Demario as if noticing how fair and somehow delicate she looked in contrast to the Italian's darkness. 'This is all very sudden, isn't it, my dear? On the occasions you have dined with me, I can't recall that you ever mentioned that you were seeing another man, least of all with the serious intention of becoming his wife. Neither can I recall that I have ever seen this young man until today.'

'That's easily explained,' she said rather faintly. 'I—I knew Rome when we were children. We—we met again some time ago and realised—oh, you know how it is, Paul. These things can happen overnight.'

'Yet I wouldn't have taken you for the impulsive type.' The wheel of a gold lighter spurted flame at the cigarette between the rather thin lips of Wineman and as he narrowed his eyes against the smoke he was measuring Rome from head to heel.

'You aren't American?' he remarked.

'I live in Naples,' Rome replied. 'I am originally from Italy, though my parents resided in the States for some years. That was when Julia and I became acquainted.'

'So it was a boy-girl romance?' Wineman drawled. 'You fell for each other in your infancy and now like Romeo and Juliet you've decided that you can't live without each other. You might have warned me that this was pending, Julia.'

'I—I'm sorry, Paul.' He was distinguished, with wings of silver at his temples. He was erudite and could talk so cleverly about so many things. So courtly mannered, and with a slight world-weary smile that crinkled his dark eyes. He was so exactly the type of man Julia had set her heart on that she just didn't know how she stood there with Rome Demario, his arm around her waist, his fingers pressing her body as if already he owned her and was letting the other man know that he no longer had any right to regard her as eligible for his attentions.

It was Paul's attentions she wanted, yet she had felt driven to commit herself to a man she despised. She was a coward. She had known all along in her heart that she couldn't submit to the instrument which would have set her free from Rome Demario. It wasn't that she felt a spark of affection for his child ... it was that all her life she had been innately reserved, with a cool-skinned shining look of cleanliness that made the very thought of abortion a defiling and wretched procedure.

Because she couldn't face it she had to let Paul Wineman out of her life ... and she had to let Rome Demario into it. The only consolation was that when she gave him the child he would release her from their marriage. He had sworn to do that, and if he broke his promise ... Julia looked at him, at his well-defined Italian profile and the shoulders he carried so well on the lean supple body.

Any other woman, she supposed, might have felt thrilled to be marrying such an attractive man, but all she felt was a burning hatred for him. He had used her like a toy without feelings and there wasn't a vestige of respect or admiration in her when he looked at her and she saw again the incredible beauty of his smoke-grey eyes. No doubt his child would have those eyes ... no doubt it would be a lovely creature, but no spark of joy at the prospect lit up in Julia's eyes.

They were like green gems in her white face, hard and cool as if never again would they melt into a truly happy smile. She would go through with the marriage and the birth, and then he had to keep his promise and let her go.

'Well,' said Paul Wineman, 'I suppose I'd better be the first to congratulate you, Julia. I wish you every happiness.'

'Thank you,' Julia said, outwardly cool ... inwardly burning.

'Are you planning to have the full show, with all the trimmings such as Verna has just enjoyed?' Paul Wineman fingered the carnation in his lapel, as if he were trying to appear more casual than he felt. Julia sensed that he was distressed and hurt beneath his well-behaved manner, but there was no real comfort she could offer him. He had admired and respected her, and she knew their friendship had been mutually pleasing to both of them. Now she felt a bleak sense of loss and blamed everything on Rome Demario. He had wrecked her chance of happiness with a man she respected and she would never forgive him for it.

'No indeed,' she replied to Paul. 'I couldn't go through all that again and I'll be perfectly satisfied to be married quietly by a justice of the peace. Verna wanted all the glamour and glory, but I certainly don't.'

'All the same,' it was Rome who spoke, 'I shall want the ceremony to take place in church.'

Julia looked at him and was about to protest when he laid a finger across her lips. 'A Catholic church, my dear. You needn't dress yourself up in satin and lace, nor invite half of New York's social register, but I must insist that a priest officiate at our marriage. I am Italian and I wouldn't feel that we were properly wed without a priest of my church. For the children's sake, *carina.*'

Julia could feel the furious protest clamouring at her lips, but apart from the fact that Paul was watching her, there was in Rome's eyes a look that warned her not to argue with him. On this issue he meant to have his way ... his eyes glittered, reminding her that the child she carried was going to be his sole responsibility. He wanted her to be in no doubt that everything he did was for the child's sake.

'Very well,' she gave a slight shrug. 'So long as it's quick and quiet. I couldn't possibly face all the fuss Verna has been through—long silk dress, bridesmaids, ushers and all the rest.'

'I'm not asking you to wear white.' Rome gazed directly into her eyes. 'A pretty suit will suffice, for we'll be flying off to Naples directly the ceremony is over. From there we travel to Campania where I live.'

'Campania?' she echoed. 'That's in the deep south, isn't it?'

He inclined his dark head and a slightly wicked smile came into his eyes. 'You didn't imagine I'd ask you to live above a gambling casino, did you? I have an estate in Campania and a house I think you might find interesting. I call it the Villa Domani.'

'Doesn't that mean "tomorrow"?' she asked.

'Yes,' he agreed. 'Because everything happens tomorrow, or we believe it is going to. The realities of today and what we anticipate for tomorrow are separated by a fine thread of excitement and longing. That's why I call my home Domani.'

'It's a romantic idea.' It was Paul Wineman who spoke. 'Yet do I understand you to say that you also run a gambling casino?'

'There are two side to my life,' Rome replied, giving the other man a slightly arrogant look. 'Julia won't be required to share the half that belongs in Naples. You look disapproving, *signore*. Do you take me for an Italian gangster? A man of the underworld who carries a gun, or to be more in keeping a stiletto up his sleeve?'

'To be quite honest with you,' Paul moved his glance from Rome to Julia, 'I wouldn't have taken you for the kind of man Miss Van Holden would be in love with.'

'Are you a great judge of these things?' Rome drawled. 'I knew Miss Van Holden when she was a small girl who liked strawberry ice-cream and blue buckled shoes. I always swore to myself that I'd marry her.'

Julia gave him a deeply startled look when he said this, erect and darkly graceful in his custom-made Italian suit. *Homme fatal!* The knowledge of what really inspired his wish to marry her was like a stiletto in her heart . . . he was Latin and long ago he had learned to hate the Van Holdens because at that time they had been rich and his mother had been poor enough to have to plead to be kept on as a cleaner in their house. Julia remembered how the Demario boy had stood there, grimly tugging at his mother's hand when she begged Grandma Van Holden not to dismiss her.

That incident, Julia knew, had given birth to a vengeance Rome was now enjoying. She saw the little pleased smile at the end of his mouth because he had so thoroughly humbled her Van Holden pride.

'And did you, Julia, wish to marry him when you were a small girl?' Paul Wineman gave her a rather quizzical smile.

'He was an arrogant boy who threw ice-cream all over

my shoes,' she replied. 'Now shall we return to the reception? I expect Verna and her husband will almost be ready to start out on their honeymoon trip.'

Julia pulled free of Rome, walking away from him, back into the room where the wedding guests were chatting in animated, smartly dressed groups, the darkly clad waiters moving among them with trays of food and drink.

It was all very lively, touched by that air of excitement that a wedding creates in the hearts of most people. Verna looked radiant in her deep-pink going away suit and the smile on her face was Julia's only consolation. At least one of the Van Holden sisters would be happy in her marriage, and those damning IOUs had long since been destroyed.

Julia walked towards her sister in order to kiss her goodbye. Only a close observer would have noticed the irony in her smile. Had she really said to Verna when they burned those gambling slips: 'There, now we can forget about Naples and everything connected with the place. It's all gone up in smoke!'

'Darling!' Verna flung her arms about Julia and hugged her. 'Thank you for my lovely wedding and all the hard work you've put into it. You are the best sister any girl could have, and soon it will be your turn to walk up the aisle with a man you adore. There's nothing quite like it. I feel like a princess!'

'You look like one.' Julia kissed her sister and smiled at the man who would now be responsible for her. 'Always be as happy, Verna, as you are today.'

'I intend to,' Verna said with confidence, her ringed hand tucked around the arm of her bridegroom. 'I'm never going to do anything that will make this man of mine think less of me than he does today. Today he thinks I'm the icing on the cake!'

Everyone laughed ... they didn't notice the frozen way

Julia was looking at the tall, dark man who stood on the edge of the crowd. He was the stranger here, the outsider, and yet he shared with her the most intimate of secrets. How shocked everyone would be if they knew she was having his baby!

CHAPTER TWO

JULIA noticed on the aircraft how the stewardesses kept glancing at Rome as they moved up and down the aisle, ensuring that the passengers were comfortable and had all they required. She felt certain they were extra concerned that he should be well taken care of, and didn't doubt that each one of them would have liked to change places with her.

She didn't think that she and Rome looked like a 'just married' couple. They weren't holding hands and looking into each other's eyes as if they couldn't wait to be alone together. They sat with a certain amount of space between them and she still wore her glove on her left hand, concealing the golden gleam of the wide-banded ring he had placed on her marriage finger twenty-four hours ago, almost gothic in design and companioned by an emerald in gold claws which weighed on her slim hand. She had tried to resist the emerald, whose clarity and cut told her it was real, but he had gripped her by the wrist there in Tiffany's and slid the ring on her finger, smiling narrowly when the assistant remarked that it matched her eyes.

'That's the idea,' Rome drawled as he wrote out the cheque. 'It's a rare combination, isn't it, a blonde with green eyes?'

'In case you're wondering,' she had said to him outside the shop, 'my hair isn't dyed.'

'I know that, Julia.' Inside the cab that drove them to the church he had smiled in a nostalgic way. 'I knew you when you were a little one, remember? Your hair was bright as a dandelion and my mother once told me that your nursemaid used to rinse it in lemon juice so it would keep its colour. It worked, eh?'

Oh yes, thought Julia, sitting there beside him on the jet, it would suit his sense of style that her fairness was a pleasing contrast to his Latin darkness. There was no denying that he was stylish, with excellent taste that was either innate or carefully cultivated. His three-piece grey suit was without fault, combined with a shirt and tie in white and grey, with golden ovals at his cuffs, matching the gold ring which had been held out to her on the prayer book and which she had to place on his marriage finger. He could, she supposed, have been taken for a member of a high class family, with the well-defined profile and patrician nose.

'Why are you called Rome?' she suddenly asked him.

He looked at her a trifle sardonically, for she hadn't spoken to him voluntarily since they had left the church as husband and wife, merely replying to his remarks as they drove to the airport and were checked in for the flight. When he had bent his tall head to kiss her mouth she had quickly turned her cheek so his kiss fell against the side of her lips. In her ivory-coloured suit and *eau-de-nil* blouse she looked as cool as her eyes upon his face.

'To remind my mother of the eternal city when she and my father left Italy to live in America,' he replied. 'There seemed more chance of him finding a good job and he worked hard so he could buy a share in a shoe business. He was unaware that one of the partners was crooked, and he was blamed for a fraud that wasn't his and sent to prison. While there he tried to defend a youth who found himself under siege by a homosexual thug, and for that my father was beaten senseless and he died in the prison hospital of a ruptured blood vessel in his inside. Of necessity my mother had to cook and clean for those who could afford to pay her for working herself half to death so I wouldn't go hungry to school with holes in my shoes.'

He broke off abruptly and took a deep drink of his champagne. 'I don't suppose you remember my mother, but in her wedding photograph she wore a lace veil and looked so lovely and eager, as if she believed that love was going to be hers all her life. I gave her my love, but how could it ever be the same as my father's? She died herself in Naples two years ago, and I am thankful that her sad life ended in the sunshine of Italy. She adored Italy and never could like America, and that was one of the reasons why I chose to make Naples my place of business. I won't make excuses for the casino, except to say that I wanted money as soon as possible. My mother had leukaemia and I was able to give her a few comfortable years before she joined my father.'

He fell quiet, his grey eyes fixed broodingly upon the champagne glass in his hand. 'The best vintage you have on board,' he had requested, and it had struck Julia that he would have liked to tell the stewardess that he was a bridegroom.

'I—I'm sorry to hear about your parents,' she said. 'But that doesn't excuse your behaviour, does it, Rome? Or doesn't it worry you very much that you've ruined my life?'

'My dear, if you represent ruin, then there should be more of it about.' His eyes were smiling, taunting her just a little as they wandered over the smooth sweep of her hair from her temples, a bright frame around the delicate charm of her face. 'You're looking particularly lovely.'

'It wouldn't suit you to have it otherwise, would it, Rome? You want women to be as stylish as the clothes you put on, so they compliment your Latin looks.'

'Do you like my looks, Julia?' He said it a trifle mockingly. 'It would be nice to know that something about me appeals to you.'

'Do you need me to like something about you, Rome?' Her cool green eyes studied his face, made striking by the good bone structure that was so entirely rooted in his Italian background. There were shadings of ruthlessness in the thrust of his cheekbones, a suggestion of great passion about the moulding of his mouth, a secretiveness in the cleft that was so exactly centred in his chin.

She had felt the power of his physical passion, so unlike anything she had imagined with a cultured, civilised man like Paul Wineman. Rome was utterly Latin, with a deep vein of southern sensuality running through him, erotic and out to enslave a woman by her senses. He would understand the dark desires a woman might feel ... might need to have gratified. At the thought Julia blushed and felt as if waves of alarm and awareness singed the very roots of her being.

This man was her husband! How could she be sure he'd abide by his promise to behave as if he were her guardian? The gold rings on her hand and the vows they'd exchanged in the church, with its stained-glass windows, its holy statues and incense, were symbols of his ownership.

'To love, honour and cherish,' he had said.

'With my body I thee—take,' she had substituted in her mind.

Julia felt a subtle sense of torment. The man she had married was ineffably his own master ... and hers. She felt it in the way he looked at her, in the way he leaned towards her, his nostrils tensing. 'You smell of lilacs,' he murmured. 'You look as if you'd been dipped in crystal like one of those classic figurines, all shining and worth a pretty penny.'

'And that pleases you, doesn't it, Rome? I now belong to you and anything you possess has to be distinctive and worth its price.' Her voice matched her outward look of cool poise, but in her mind, and her body, she was remembering how he had swept her up in his arms as if she were weightless and how warm his skin had felt when he pressed her to his brown flesh hardened by the Italian sun. Rome was flesh and blood all the way through!

'Are you very rich?' she asked. 'Have you made heaps of dollars out of those fools who gamble at your tables? I expect you have, you're that sort of man. But something puzzles me, Rome. I thought gambling was controlled by the Godfathers, those dark men from Sicily who lay down the laws where gaming is concerned—and other activities of a sinful nature.'

'You're asking if I'm a member of the Brotherhood?' He looked at her in silence a moment, and then softly laughed. 'It's always the assumption, isn't it, *carina*? But as it happens life takes odd twists and turns. I told you, didn't I, that my father died as a direct result of defending a young man in prison. That young man eventually became one of the Dons of great power and he is a friend of mine, but he isn't in any way my boss. I run my own casino in Naples because of his friendship, but I run it regardless of the Brotherhood, who would never dare touch me because of Vitale's regard for me. It is in human nature to gamble ... just as it's in the nature of the human race to eat and drink ... to love and hate. I run a good establishment. No one gets really hurt.'

'No one?' she murmured. 'You can say that to my face?'

He swept his grey eyes over her, taking in the suit that was slightly open to reveal the silk-chiffon of her blouse, on its lapel a single orchid pinned with a little tiger whose eyes shimmered green as her own. 'If I hurt you, baby, it doesn't show.'

'I have feelings,' she rejoined. 'I suppose you think because you're good-looking and well-bathed, what you did to me bears no relationship to the back alley variety of assault? I had little defence against you. You're as strong as an ox!'

'My first compliment from my bride,' he mocked. 'I'll treasure it.'

'I'd tell you to go to the devil, Rome, only I know you're there already.' She smiled sweetly as she said it and in reply he raised his champagne glass to her.

'Do you think we'll always be as happy as we are right now, Julia?'

'Always?' she echoed, and as he continued to look at her, she felt goose bumps rising on her skin, especially her arms and the base of her spine, tingling cold and yet hot as if dry ice had been dropped down the back of her blouse.

'Always is a long time, Rome, if you're getting ideas just because of that ceremony yesterday morning. Why was it in church? You aren't a religious man, you take too many gambles.'

'It would have pleased my mother. She wanted me to marry so she could be a grandmother. Italian people like the solid continuation of the family; they enjoy seeing children around the house, hearing their laughter and seeing in their faces the family likeness. It makes death seem but a door through which to step, with part of you still alive. She would have been pleased about the child.'

'Is that why you married me?' Julia asked quietly. 'It is only the child you want, isn't it? I—I need to know.'

'Of course I want my child.' His lashes seemed to darken his eyes, the lowering of his lids giving him both a sinister and a sensual look. 'I've already made that perfectly plain, have I not, Julia?'

'So long as I know, Rome. I don't want to stay married to you for longer than is necessary.'

'The child will be as much yours as mine, Julia. You may love it regardless of me.'

'I could never love any part of you,' she said scornfully. 'The kind of men I like behave like gentlemen, and for all your fine clothes and your villa in Campania, you're basically a ruthless, vindictive brute who pretends to care for the memory of your mother. If you had any real respect for women, I wouldn't be here right now, married to you and hating every minute of it.'

'Do you mind lowering your voice?' he said pleasantly. 'I don't care to have it broadcast that I have a shrew for a wife.'

'I'd like to tell the world what I have for a husband.' Her eyes blazed into his. 'I'm no sweet and adoring Italian girl for you to order about, *signore*. Respect and adoration have to be earned, and all I have for you is aversion. It's only because you're tall that I look up to you, but to me you'll always be low class.'

'*Grazie*.' He inclined his handsome head, his lashes still dark across the centres of his eyes. 'With a shrew for a mother and a brute for a father the pair of us can expect to have a charming infant!'

'It's your fault there's to be an infant at all,' she rejoined bitterly. 'Nothing could be harder to bear than having your child inside me. A child should be made with love, and this one is already branded with hate.'

'Not mine,' he said quickly. 'It wasn't one of the worst experiences of my life, having you in my arms. You're very lovely——'

'For God's sake stop it!' She flung a hand over her eyes and turned her head away from him, gazing out blindly at the sheer white clouds bouncing by in a sky of incredible blueness. The plane dropped a little, then rose again and her stomach heaved. No ... no, she mustn't be sick. Not in front of Rome. It was bad enough that she felt so queasy when she first woke up, the physical proof that she was bearing his child, so mortifying when she looked in the mirror and saw her own pallor and the tiny beads of sweat on her skin. And there would be more to suffer! Her body would fill out and grow heavy, and that unwanted burden inside her would sap her energy and take the youthful spring out of her walk and the lustre out of her hair. She would look horrible, and then would come the painful, sweating business of giving birth!

A shudder went through her body. It would be different if she wanted the baby ... if she loved the man who had given it to her.

'Are you feeling all right?' His fingers closed upon her arm. 'Come, Julia, if you wish to be sick——'

'Shut up and go to hell!' she said fiercely, pulling free of his touch. 'I don't want you or your concern. Leave me alone!'

'You know I can't do that, so don't be childish, Julia. What has to be, will be, and we have to make the best of it.'

'All right for you, Rome. Your body hasn't been violated!'

'*Santo Dio*, do you have to say such things?'

'Do they hurt, Rome?' She turned to look at him curiously. 'Can you actually feel them pricking your insensitive skin? I'd never stop saying them if I thought that was possible. It would be a gratifying way to pass the time I must spend with you.'

'I won't take too much goading,' he warned her. 'Push me too far and you already know what happens.'

'Yes, Rome, you use brute force. I imagine it's in you. The Romans were never very gentle, were they? Look what they did to the Sabine women, not to mention those poor devils they fed to the lions. Isn't it true that we are what our forebears have been?'

'No doubt the Van Holdens kept slaves for years,' he said sarcastically. 'Your grandmother certainly took it for granted that other people were around to take her orders. But maybe you wouldn't be aware of that. She obviously spoiled you and your sister and turned the pair of you into pretty little dolls, too rare to be touched by human hands. I remember the boys at your sister's party, wearing kid gloves to handle the little girls in their satin dresses. Kids who grow up thinking there are two types of women, those they must treat like art objects, and those they pay for an hour's fun.'

'You'd know all about that, no doubt,' Julia said coldly.

'On the contrary,' he gave a soft laugh, 'I've never had to pay a woman.'

'How flattering for your ego!'

'No, my dear, I flatter women by treating them as such. I wouldn't insult them by presuming they have feelings as fragile as glass, and that only the male of the species has senses that can give him pleasure. That's why the girls of your class develop into dissatisfied harridans, it's because they've never known what it feels like to be treated as sensual women, with desires that need the human touch. They become brides in clouds of lace and silk, and then are initiated into wifehood with swift cool politeness by a bridegroom who believes that if his bride has social pedigree then she has no sex.'

Rome lit one of his dark Italian cigars and quirked an eyebrow at her. Julia knew what he meant ... to him all women were the same, whether from her background or the backstreets of Naples. He had never treated any of them with swift cool politeness when he took them in his arms.

'You're quite the Lothario, aren't you?' she said, a certain fine disdain showing on her face. 'I prefer a man who has more of an objective in life than proving his machismo at every opportunity.'

'Like strolling around art galleries and writing literate pieces for the art magazines?' he drawled. 'I doubt if even you, my dear, would have found that very thrilling after a while.'

'What do you mean?' she asked. 'I enjoyed my work and people I met in the course of it——'

'Wineman the art critic in particular, eh? What does it feel like to be kissed by someone who looks as if he has pale blue ink in his veins?'

'Paul isn't the sort who grabs hold of a woman and forces himself upon her. He's a gentleman—and if you don't mind I'd like to change the subject. I find it offensive discussing my good friends with you.'

'You're a bit of a snob, Julia, but that's to be expected when you grew up in the care of a woman like Blanche Van Holden. It's a wonder she didn't ruin you entirely.'

'She left that to you,' Julia retorted. 'If anyone has had a bad effect on my character, then it's you, Rome. I never knew I had an edge to my temper until I met you.'

'Temper in a woman is like garlic in food, fine so long as there isn't too much of it.' His eyes were amused through the smoke of his cigar. 'I think I'm able to control your temper, *carina*. If it gets too shrewish, then I'll put you over my knee and apply a little paddling to your backside.'

'You wouldn't dare,' she gasped. 'Don't forget——'

The smile in his eyes deepened at the way she bit her lip, the colour rising from the neck opening of her blouse to the smooth curve of her cheekbones.

'Pregnant women aren't all that fragile until the final few weeks,' he said. 'I have a stretch of beach at Domani and you'll be able to swim, and I daresay ride. You're a very fit girl. Most of the activities of a bride will be within your scope, so there should be no need for either of us to feel deprived.'

Julia felt an alarming throb of her pulse when he included himself in the activities she could enjoy until her figure became too ungainly. There seemed a double meaning in his words and she saw the little glint in his eyes when she searched them, as if he mocked her for an innocent fool.

'Can't the master of Domani swim and ride and enjoy some dancing?' he asked. 'The *terrazza* of the villa is above the beach and it's quite romantic there on a moonlit night and wide enough for two to dance to the music of the stereo. I know you learned to dance as a child. Then, of course, you were partnered by polite little boys wearing kid gloves. I wonder how you'll like me for a partner? I'm told I dance quite well.'

The lean grace and suppleness of his body gave proof of that, but it wasn't curiosity about his dancing that occupied Julia's mind. There had been some other meaning in his words, and the acceleration of her pulse made her feel breathless. She twisted the rings on her finger, symbols of his status as a husband ... a man who had already proved conclusively that he could be deaf to a woman's pleading when passion held sway over him. Now he had a legal right to her, and it was there in his bold features that he would hardly live with a woman on any basis but a fundamental one.

She had been foolishly innocent to believe his talk about behaving like a guardian to her! A naïve fool to accept his word that it was only the child he wanted!

'Are those rings hurting you?' He reached out and drew off her glove, the sun through the window catching the facets of the emerald and making it glow as he studied her hand. 'They seem to fit all right, but you've been twisting them about as if you would like to wrench them off. I'm not going to allow that, Julia. You are now my wife and you'd better make the best of it.'

'You were stringing me along,' she said tensely. 'You never meant to be a—a sort of guardian to me. It was your intention all along to have your money's worth when you bought me these rings. Damn you, Rome! I didn't dream I'd ever come up against a—a devil like you! I truly didn't think it possible to despise a man so much—you're everything I thought you, every name I called you that night in Naples. You schemed to have Verna lose money at your gaming tables and if I hadn't come to the casino on her behalf I expect she'd be the one paying the price I'm now paying!'

'No, my dear.' He held her gaze as firmly as he held her hand. 'I saw you one day in the market place at Naples buying a wickerwork bag from a vendor and right away I knew who you were. The girl in the rose-coloured dress, shyly holding out a strawberry ice to a boy who couldn't believe the dandelion hair was real but whose raging pride made him drop the ice-cream all over your best shoes. Great big tears filled your eyes and I was about to swallow my pride and say I was sorry when your grandmother came storming out after you and made my mother pay for those tears—tears I was suddenly angry about because I knew you must have lots of shoes in your closet. Because of those shoes my mother had to get down on her knees and scrub the corridors in an office building and come home at night with pains in her bones from all that kneeling on cold damp floors.'

He drew a deep breath, his nostrils tightening and looking chiselled. 'I used to watch her taking off her thin-soled shoes and peeling off her damp stockings and I felt a hatred of the Van Holdens in my bones. They had so much and we had so little—it seemed to me an enormity of injustice that my pretty mother should have to work so hard while your grandmother and two small girls were waited on hand and foot, every whim and fancy catered for, with ice-cream to eat whenever you wanted it. So try to understand a little what I felt, Julia, when you came to my casino that night and asked me to give you those IOUs as if they were your due because you were a Van Holden. You stood there, a grown-up version of the little girl in the big house, looking at me with *eau-de-nil* eyes, telling me I had purposely allowed your sister to gamble and lose.

'If you hadn't called me names, Julia, the outcome might have been different, but when you revile an Italian you take the good name of his parents as well, and mine were very dear to me. You asked for what happened——'

'Asked for it?' she gasped. 'Is that the excuse you've made for yourself, that I made you misbehave yourself and now like a proper Italian you've done me the honour of marrying me! And being so honoured I'm now to expect endless repeats of what took place in Naples?'

Tormentedly she tried to break his hold on her, but it was unbreakable and her hand twisted and turned in an impossible effort to be free of him.

'You'll only hurt yourself,' he warned. 'When we reach Campania you'll feel differently about all this. There's something in the air, especially at night when the sea below the villa window is filled with whisperings and the lanterns of the fishing boats bob on the water. Then you can smell the lemon trees and the tang of camphor and cypress. We'll take supper on the *terrazza* and you'll feel the romance of it all getting into your blood. You aren't as cool as you pretend to be. You need affection, for your own sake and for the child——'

'Affection?' She gave a bitter little laugh. 'You can't possibly imagine that I'm panting for your kisses?'

'Not right now,' he agreed, 'but Campania isn't called the place of romantic passion for nothing. Wait until you've been there a while and the soft warm air and the southern music get to you. There are sleeping fires in you, Julia.'

'But not for you,' she said fiercely. 'Whatever you do to me, Rome, you can't touch my heart. Whatever you get from me, you'll have to take. I'll just be paying for my bed and board and whenever you come to me, you'll be collecting your rent money.'

'Santo Dio,' he smiled thinly, 'I would never have believed that such a soft pair of lips could say such acrimonious things.'

'I have my pride,' Julia tilted her chin, 'and you won't drag that down to your *scugnizzo* level!'

He caught his breath and suddenly his grip was like a vice that threatened to crush her fingers, pressing the rings into her flesh and bone until her lips whitened with the pain. He watched her as she endured the pain, then he slowly relaxed his grip, releasing her hand so it dropped limply into her lap.

A stewardess appeared at his side, smiling into his eyes as she informed him that lunch was about to be served and what did he and his wife fancy to drink with it. He asked what was on the menu and ordered an appropriate wine without consulting Julia, who sat there feeling the ebbing pain in her fingers. Body and soul she throbbed with resentment as the deep timbre of Rome's voice mingled with the girl's lighter tones. Resentfully she didn't want to eat the food and drink the wine that would nourish his child. She wished she could be rid of it ... that way she'd really hurt Rome Demario and his almighty Latin pride in making a Van Holden girl pregnant. He liked the idea of being father to a child in whose veins was élite American blood ... it combined vengeance with the egotistical pleasure of taking with him to Campania a wife who was obviously a lady.

At that moment Julia's feelings were less than ladylike. She surged to her feet and pushed past Rome. 'I need to go and wash,' she said icily. 'I feel grubby.'

It was the emphasis she laid on the word that made him narrow his eyes as he rose to his feet and made it easier for her to reach the aisle.

'Don't take too long,' he said. 'Lunch is about to be served and you must be feeling hungry.'

'Must I?' she retorted. 'How clever of you to be always so sure of my feelings!'

She swept away from him, head held high as she made for the powder room, not unaware that several male heads turned to watch her progress. It was her hair which attracted attention; being natural in its fairness it had a shining look that combined with the fine silken texture of her skin and the Nile green of her eyes made her a very attractive young woman. Her ivory suit was also in good taste and her long slender legs and fine-boned ankles were encased in cobweb silk and two-toned lizard shoes. Her handbag matched the shoes and altogether she was eye-catching, though it was doubtful if anyone guessed she was a bride.

A bride, she knew, was expected to look starry-eyed, but when she gazed at herself in the mirror of the powder-room she saw that her eyes were shadowed within the frame of her lashes and the arch of her brows, which were naturally darker than her hair. The only radiant thing about her was the emerald on her hand, shooting its green fire as she ran a comb through the wings of hair that smoothly upcurled on her shoulders.

Julia wondered what Verna's reaction had been when she received in Paris the wire which informed her that she was now related by marriage to the Italian gambler who she innocently believed had presented her with the IOUs which could have had an adverse effect on her own marriage. Verna might find the situation rather romantic, Julia thought, seeing reflected in the mirror the cynical twist of her lips, but her husband and his family would hardly be delighted. A man such as Paul Wineman would have suited them as an in-law, but not Rome Demario. He was so obviously foreign and involved not in law, banking or the arts, but in a more blatant form of commerce.

Julia recalled the women she had seen playing at the casino, heavily painted, the sparkle of their jewels rivalling the gambling lustre in their eyes. It wouldn't trouble Rome's conscience if such women lost money at his tables, but Julia found unforgivable the way he had used Verna in order to lure herself into his trap.

That was what her marriage felt like . . . she was so firmly caught in the trap he had laid that there seemed only one way of escaping from it, and that was to try quite deliberately to lose this child he had set his heart on.

She placed a hand on her midriff, pressing upon herself until she felt the slight swell that betrayed the presence of the infant. Rome was the only one who wanted it . . . the spoils of the battle fought in the luxury of his bedroom above the gaming rooms of the white-stoned casino set in a palm court on the Neapolitan waterfront.

Rome had said that when they arrived at the Villa Domani she could swim and ride; both were energetic activities and this was her first pregnancy. Being a man he probably didn't realise that a first baby was more easily lost than a second or third, especially if the mother was psychologically opposed to bearing it.

Julia dropped her compact and comb into her handbag, smoothed the jacket of her suit, and emerged from the powder-room. As she made her way back to Rome there was a defiant little flame burning in her eyes. She heard the intake of his breath when she pressed past him into her seat; he had caught the scent of her freshly applied face powder and as she sat down Julia smiled quietly to herself. He was vulnerable in his own way, this tawny Italian with his southern sensuality, and the next time they battled he would be the one who got wounded.

Lunch was served and Julia suddenly found that she was hungry. She tucked into butterfly steak with baby peas, potatoes and gravy. She enjoyed the individual pudding with syrup which followed, and had two glasses of red wine. She was aware that Rome sat there looking suavely amused by her appetite, a lazy droop to his eyelids. He made no comment, but when coffee was served he remarked to the stewardess that his wife had very much enjoyed the cuisine on board the aircraft. Julia noticed the way he said 'my wife', a definite note of possessiveness in his voice.

'That's nice to know, sir.' The girl's eyes flicked Julia's hair and face and the orchid on the lapel of her suit. Her gaze dropped to the emerald which sparkled its facets on to the smooth suiting, and it was obvious to Julia that she was envious and would have liked to be possessed by a man whose looks and style made him seem the epitome of Latin charm.

'When is touchdown?' he enquired.

The girl glanced at her wristwatch and said they would be landing at Naples in exactly one hour and twenty-five minutes. 'I'm pleased you've enjoyed the flight, sir. Will you be returning to New York?'

He smiled and shook his head. 'We have a villa in Campania and at this time of the year it's very pleasant there. The sea is very blue and it will be good for my wife to get away from the tall buildings of her native city, where to me the air always feels as if it's been put through a pressure steamer. I couldn't live anywhere else but in Italy.'

'It is very exciting.' The girl was looking at him as if she really meant that he was. 'Things Latin do have that certain charisma.'

'Do they?' He drew Julia's left hand towards him and enfolded it in his own. 'I wonder if my wife agrees with you? Do you, my dear?'

He looked into her eyes and she gave him back a cool look. 'Whatever you say, Rome. I know Italian husbands like to have their opinions supported and their instructions obeyed. It oils their ego and makes them smooth, I expect.'

The stewardess looked as if she didn't know whether to disapprove of the remark or smile at it. Her eyes went automatically to Rome, as if to take a lead from him.

'My wife has a droll sense of humour.' His expression was sardonic. 'She's also a little shy and likes to hide her feelings from people. I'm the only one permitted to know exactly what she thinks of me.'

'I'm sure she thinks you're——' The girl broke off, blushing. 'If you want more coffee, or anything, *signore*, just give me a call. I'll be only too happy to oblige you.'

'I'm sure she would,' Julia laughed softly when the stewardess moved away to attend to her other passengers. 'That girl would love to be sitting here cuddled up real close to you. She thinks you're a charmer, with loads of machismo and such perfect manners. You really know how to put on a good act, don't you, Rome? With your talent for charm and your dashing looks you should have gone to Hollywood and taken over where Tyrone Power left off.'

'You're such a sweet-faced bitch, Julia.' He said it with a smile, and bending over her put a kiss against her cheekbone. 'For the benefit of the stewardess,' he murmured. 'She's determined to believe we're a very romantic couple.'

'If I'm a bitch, Rome, then take the credit for it.' Julia gave him a cool look, but his lips had left their warmth against her skin, reminding her of other kisses he had made her accept, of being helpless in a pair of arms whose bronzed strength could still send shivers up and down her spine. Her eyes dwelt on his shoulders in the grey suiting that was tailored smoothly to their power. Alone at the villa with him she would have little defence against whatever he desired of her, and neither her reluctance nor her lack of affection would prevent him from having his way with her, no more than they had done at the casino.

Julia looked into his eyes and saw the devil fires burning there, lit long ago from his boyhood rage and now a hundred times more inflammable in the adult Rome Demario. She tried to remember the boy he had been, but the memory was lost in the man he had become.

'Will you really enjoy being married to a woman who hates you?' she asked, with a cool politeness.

'It could prove to be a fascinating experience,' he rejoined. 'It will provide me with the task of taming you, won't it, my lovely? After all, what fun is there in having a filly who accepts the bridle without kicking up her heels? And what kind of challenge is there in a sea without unpredictable currents and high tides? You know me for a gambler, Julia. I enjoy staking my bet on an outside chance.'

'And do you always win?' she enquired.

'Some of the time.' He drew his fingers down the smoothness of her hair. 'To think Rome Demario can do this to the little girl who always looked so neat and prim! There were times when I longed to take you into the back streets where

I played so I could bring you back to your grandmother with street dirt on your face and tangles in your well-combed hair, and maybe a hole in your white socks.'

Julia jerked her head away from his touch. 'Eventually you managed to drag me through the dirt,' she said coldly. 'Had my grandmother been still alive she'd have had you bullwhipped.'

'You mean you'd have told her?' He quirked a black eyebrow. 'Somehow that doesn't sound like you, Julia. When you left me that morning in Naples you meant to bury the memory of me deep as a stone dropped into the Long Island sound. You wouldn't have told a soul about that night. You just wanted to wipe it out as if it had never been. What did you do when you realised you had a memento from the bad-mannered Italian boy? Did you burst into tears, or toss your hairbrush through a window?'

'I cursed the very thought of you.' Her fingers tensed and curled as she looked into his dark handsome face, wanting to make him bleed, wanting to make him curl into an agonised heap on the floor, where she had lain for a long time wishing that despair could lead quietly and quickly to death itself.

Then as if he saw in her face some residue of the despair she had felt, he said quietly: 'You are safe now, Julia. Matters have been adjusted, and no one knows except the two of us that our marriage was a necessity.'

'You promised me that our marriage would be——' She bit her lip, for the words would sound archaic and yet she had to say them. 'You promised it would be in name only.'

'Have some sense, Julia.' He frowned and flipped open his cigar case. 'How can you expect a man to behave like a monk with a woman who has his name and is to bear his child? I know I'm every sort of villian in your eyes, capable of every sort of lowdown trick, but I had to make you marry me. No way was I going to allow my child to be removed from you as if it was garbage. That baby will be born, and I'm too much flesh and blood not to want the woman who carries it for me.'

He shrugged and applied a flame to his cigar. 'Love is good for a woman. It gives her a glow.'

'Love?' Julia looked at him in total incredulity. 'Do you know what you are, Rome Demario?'

'A man, *carina*?' Smoke drifted lazily from his lips. 'You tell me what you think I am.'

'A devil who'd break every commandment in the book just for the hell of it! I hope you never showed your true self to your poor mother!'

Through the drifting cigar smoke he stared at Julia and suddenly he had a brooding look. 'I don't discuss my mother with a Van Holden. I've told you how she died, now we'll let her rest.'

Julia bit her lip and turned her head away from him. She gazed out upon the sky where the great balls of cloud looked solid enough to bounce. Soon they would be over Naples, and her hand clenched against her body. Rome wanted this child with a kind of passion she couldn't fully understand ... unless it gave him a cruel kind of satisfaction because he had forced it upon her.

She sat there, resolve hardening in her to deny him the ultimate joy in his vendetta against the Van Holdens. He could only feel that when he held the baby in his arms ... what would he feel if she lost it? Would agony clutch at his insides and drag him down on his knees in abject misery?

How that would pleasure her, to see that happen to Rome Demario!

'Soon we'll be landing.' He reached up for her travelling coat of smooth cashmere, with a deep velvet collar, expensive and perfectly tailored and bought in place of the fur coat she had refused adamantly to accept. 'There's enough cruelty and destructiveness in this world,' she had said meaningly.

He assisted her into the coat and flicked her hair out of the collar. 'You'd look stunning in mink, the dark shining variety,' he murmured. 'I know a furrier in Naples——'

'From whom you've bought furs for your other conquests?' she broke in. 'No, thank you! I only accepted this coat at your insistence but I won't wear fur and be a walking advertisement for the suffering and slaughter inflicted on poor dumb animals. I don't expect *you* to understand my point of view, you're too used to fleecing human beings to have any mercy for mere animals.'

'Always you find something flattering to say to your husband, don't you, *mia*?' He gripped her shoulders; there was a menacing smile in his eyes and the cleft in his chin looked deep and dark. 'Fools and their money are easily parted and if I didn't rake it in at my tables someone else would. Look where honour and trust in others put my father! Believe me, Julia, I learned my lessons very young and I've never forgotten them ... expect very little from other people and you won't be disappointed, for it isn't the meek who inherit the earth, it's those with the gall to take the plums off the tree before they fall to the ground.'

'Rome,' she sighed, 'you're a real cynic.'

'I'm no saint,' he agreed, 'but I know how to treat a woman who fires my blood.'

'Yes,' her face was pensive, 'I learned how well in Naples.'

'See Naples and die, eh?' he mocked.

'You killed something in me, Rome.'

'A girlish idealism maybe. A belief in shining knights who rescue maidens in distress. Did you come to the casino hoping to find a modern equivalent who'd regard you as a damsel in distress?'

'The moment I saw you——!' She clamped her lip and shook her head. The angry hurt boy had become a man, eyes glinting with the shared memories as they swept up and down her grown up figure.

'Strange we should meet again, eh? What was between us was unfinished and incomplete, and being Latin I believe in the machinations of fate. Had my parents stayed in Italy instead of going to the States I might now be working contentedly in a vineyard or running a *ristorante*, and you would no doubt have married into the social register and remained unaware of my existence. As it is, Julia, *che sera, sera*.'

'Fasten your safety belts, please.' The stewardess was leaning over Rome, giving him a shy but inviting smile. Julia wondered if the girl hoped for some signal from him that he would like to see her again, and she watched him as if hoping for his betrayal.

'Napoli,' he said. 'It's where I met my wife.'

'Then you must be longing to get there, sir.'

'We are, aren't we, my dear?' He directed a slight smile at Julia.

'I can't wait,' she said cynically, and as the aircraft began to lose height, she felt as if her heart was sinking as well.

CHAPTER THREE

The late afternoon was sheened with a raw gold haze, lovely and just a little melancholy. The vine-terraced hills had a blue look and trees made lacy smudges of shadow, and here and there were women shrouded in black, making their way home after a day in the fields. It was like another world to Julia, with an unreal quality to it, for here long ago in this lush countryside the Romans had built their fine white villas when they retired from their campaigns or their seats in the Senate.

The noisy, teeming city of Naples had been left far behind and she listened to the easy purring of the sleek Maserati as it took the steep gradient with its spectacular views over sea and land. Rome's car had been garaged at the casino while he flew to New York to attend her sister's wedding and of necessity they had gone there by cab from the airport. Seeing the place once more, with the broad palm trees green against the white walls, had brought back memories that made it difficult for Julia to enjoy the drive to Campania.

Everything would have been so different had she been a carefree tourist, with nothing to mar the journey for her. If she could have relaxed she might have found really fascinating the natural beauty of it all, with Vesuvius smouldering over the ruins of Pompeii, and below the curving, spectacular highway the deep waters of Lake Averno, where the boats to Hades were said to glide when darkness fell.

Rome swung the wheel of the car and cornered with all the expertise of an Italian who took pride in a speedy, well-constructed car. He wore hogskin driving gloves, and the interior of the Maserati, upholstered in fire-red suede, bore all the signs that the car hadn't come off the production line but had been custom-built to Rome's demanding specifications. Julia's seat felt as comfortable as a lounger, and across her body a leather strap was fastened by a buckle much smoother and easier than others she had worn.

She admired the precision and quality of Rome's driving with the detachment of a stranger. From a deprived boy he had certainly grown into a man of initiative, with a look of style and culture about him. Few people would have guessed that the sophistication concealed a creature as dangerous as a tiger; sleek and merciless in dealing with his prey. People would have scoffed that a woman in a beautiful cashmere coat, wearing on her hand a costly emerald ring, thought of herself as this man's prey. But she saw it in every glance he gave her, centred deep in his brilliant eyes. Heard its undertone in his voice when he spoke about the wild grandeur of this part of Italy where neither the land nor the people had been really tamed, not even in Roman times.

They sped along its winding, dazzling coast until when the sun started to decline he told her that they were within a few miles of the villa.

The house of tomorrow, Julia reflected, where far from familiar surroundings and people she knew and trusted, she must live with a man she distrusted with every nerve in her body. Her fingers played restlessly with the emerald, companioned by the solid band of gold that symbolised the bonds of marriage. Frightened and anxious about the future, she had believed Rome when he said their marriage would be but a necessity. She had clung to an illusion and now she had to face the reality. Without loving her, Rome was possessive of her and his most fleeting glance or touch was sufficient to convey his sense of ownership. Her slim white shape and the child she carried were his, just as this car was his, and the villa above its own stretch of beach.

I take and hold could have been the motto of this man who had known what it was like to be poor; to be the outsider while others belonged to a charmed inner circle of privilege and plenty. Julia knew she was symbolic to him of that charmed circle and that made her all the more to be desired ... and tormented. The girl in the rose-coloured party dress, with the bright hair and the buckles shining on her shoes. The little girl in the big house, who would now belong to him in his own big house.

They came suddenly to a driveway that snaked along an avenue of cypress trees, their limbs twisted with age, darkened by time and weather. A tall pair of gates glided open automatically, responding to an ingenious gadget fixed into the dashboard of the Maserati. Stone pillars stood at either side of the gates, with the heraldic figures of twin falcons upon them, one with wings outstretched, the other with its wings folded.

'Almost like the Borgias,' Julia couldn't resist saying. 'When I look at you, Rome, I wonder if there's some connection.'

'It's kind of you to select one of the most notorious families in Italian history, my dear.'

'They were so handsome and terrible, Rome, that the comparison is irresistible. Your bone structure can be seen in the portraits of the Renaissance.'

'That might almost be a compliment, Julia.'

'I don't deny your looks, Rome. You're probably the best looking man I'm ever likely to meet, and I expect you've known for years that you can have your way with most of the women you meet. Some women do have a tendency to prefer the wrappings to the contents.'

'But you aren't one of them, eh?'

'I think you've discovered that for yourself, *signore.* If your character matched your profile, then you might be straightforward instead of devious. When you come to think of it, the way people look should reflect their inner selves.'

'Then you'd be an angel, my dear.'

The car made a turn and there was the villa rising against the sunset, its rose-coloured walls giving it a beauty that made Julia press a hand to her mouth as if to suppress her instant need to say it was haunting, entrancing, like a painting from out of the past. At one side of it a tower curled high like a serpent from the sea, capped by oval black tiles rising into a peak.

Julia felt the quick beating of her heart and knew herself mysteriously charmed by that slim, dark-capped tower, its narrow windows aflame in the sunset.

'A dramatic welcome for you to Domani.' Rome was holding open the car door beside her and caught in a kind of spell she placed her hand in his and was drawn out on to the stone flags of the forecourt. The moment was so acutely strange that she gripped his hand so tightly that she felt the tiny hairs on the backs of his fingers.

'It's a house of yesterday, not tomorrow,' she murmured, and as they stood there the ravished sky grew darker and the sun sank out of sight. Cypress leaves rustled and a breath of ocean wafted across the forecourt, where at the centre stood a fountain with gods and nymphs cavorting in marble.

'It's quite a *palagio.*' Julia glanced at Rome and his features had a bold dark clarity which should have been set off by the dark velvet men had worn at the time this villa was built. It was pictorial in its design and ambience. It radiated an air of romantic seclusion, as if meant for a couple who came here for romantic reasons. There was no romance in the reason she came here with Rome, and her glance was drawn back to the tower, symbolic of captivity.

'Are you wondering if I'm going to lock you up in my sea tower?' Rome enquired drily. 'Doubtless it may have been used for that purpose in days gone by, but I use it for my den. It's very secluded and relaxing up there, but not very popular with my servants who don't like climbing all those stairs. They wind upwards in a spiral.'

'Was it the tower that made you buy this place?' Julia asked.

'That and the jacarandas in the gardens at the rear. I call them my blue trees.' Rome tilted back his head and took a deep breath of air into his lungs. 'This is the true smell of Italy, the sea and the sap in the trees and vines, extracted by the sun but not apparent until the day cools down. I want my child to be born here, where the air is good to breathe; where there are trees to climb and rocks and sand to play on. He or she will never know what it's like to play in city streets where there is garbage in the gutters, and drunken men in doorways, and painted women who sell themselves for a few dollars. The noise and stench and foul talk were part of my life, and I sometimes sit alone in the tower and recall myself as a youth, needing to know how to use my fists in those rough streets, needing to be part of a gang because anyone alone got beaten up, finding dance-hall escape on Saturday nights until I realised that I could escape altogether if I used my wits.'

Rome paused and looked about him in the gathering dusk, his hands still holding Julia's. 'I escaped from all that and found Domani. I have a painting of it in my office at the casino to remind me that it's always here, waiting for me, a reality and not just the dream of a boy in a New York slum.'

When he spoke like that Julia felt an instinctive sympathy for the boy he had been ... the boy long lost in the man. She had known that boy, with his thin young face which showed signs even then of becoming not only striking but distinctive. She remembered the gravity of his grey eyes and the way the dark pupils seemed to her childish imagination to look like black velvet. She had one day remarked to her nurse Lucie that she thought the Demario boy quite beautiful, but weren't boys supposed to be plainer than girls? Julia had thought herself a plain little girl because she had straight hair and eyes the colour of the green marbles she and Verna played with. Verna was the pretty one because her hair was wavy and a deeper gold colour, rather like the daffodils in Grandma's big garden.

There had been no dirt in the gutters of the street they lived on. Nor did Julia hear any bad language until she went away to finishing school where one of the girls used to say 'damn it' out of earshot of the Misses Delaine who ran the school, where charm and the social graces were learned, along with French and Italian.

Julia realised that Rome had no idea she spoke quite fluent Italian, and she decided not to tell him. It made a bond between people when they shared the ability to speak together in a foreign language, and Julia wanted to keep as much distance as possible between Rome and herself.

'No two people could be more opposite than you and I,' he remarked, 'but that's how it should be with a man and a woman. It adds an edge to the relationship, makes unpredictable their reactions to what may arise in their everyday life. I wouldn't want a woman I could read like a copy of *Vogue*.'

'I prefer a man who hasn't a Machiavellian mind,' Julia rejoined. 'With you I feel as if I'm treading on quicksand. There's no feeling of stability ... it's as if I've been led astray from a trusted path on to one that twists and turns and makes me constantly nervous of what lies ahead. The unpredictable doesn't appeal to me! I prefer a straightforward life and people to match!'

'How dull, Julia,' he mocked. 'How unexciting to have life written out like a menu, with each event for the day marked out in prim and proper order.'

'That's the sort of person I am, Rome, prim and properly brought up. What you've led me into is a kind of—of bad dream. I want to wake up and find that none of it is true. That I'm not your wife . . . that I'm not going to have your child!'

'You aren't sleeping or dreaming.' He caught her by the shoulders and brought her close to him, so she felt the hard warmth and reality of his body against hers. 'Not now you aren't, though in many ways you were a sleeping beauty before I woke you up. Life can't be run as if it's a kitsch article in a smart magazine which professes to know all the answers and supplies only advertising. Between us we have a living bond of flesh and blood, bone and marrow, growing in you as I hold you and feel you against me. Doesn't it thrill you, Julia, the mystery and wonder of it, that together we have made a small piece of humanity? Have you ice-water in your veins that you can't feel any pleasure in what a lovely, clever, exciting thing your body is?'

'That's all you think about!' She flung him a tormented look. 'That's all I am to you, a body—a machine that's in the process of fashioning a replica of yourself. Do you gaze in the mirror and imagine a daughter with your perfect Italian face, or a son with your wide shoulders and ruthless ego? Do you have plans to make him into a gambler and a seducer?'

'You will stop what you are saying!' Rome's eyes were suddenly so furious that Julia felt as if the strength drained out of her legs, leaving her limp in the grip of his hands. 'How dare you speak to me in such a way? Who do you suppose you are? Being the granddaughter of Blanche Van Holden doesn't make you superior to any girl in the village nearby. You are merely a female in trouble, and a fortunate one who has a man willing enough to supply you with a wedding ring. Do you imagine I'd want you if you weren't carrying my child? I might have intimated to the effete Paul Wineman that I always wished to marry you, but in truth you're a frigid little madam, with a sarcastic tongue in your head and a way of looking through a man that makes me want to spank your backside until you can't sit down on it. You look like a woman, Julia, but you're really a statue, and I already have enough of those around my swimming-pool. I don't plan to have one in my bedroom!'

'Your bedroom is the last place I plan to be in,' she retorted, with more defiance than conviction.

He smiled in the dusk light, a brief glimmer of strong white teeth. 'We say in Italy that a woman with temper in her is a woman with passion in her, so there may be hope for you yet.'

'You're the one that's hopeful,' she flared. 'I didn't beg of you to marry me—you know what I intended to do and if I let you talk me into this fiasco it's because I confused your word of honour with that of a man like Paul. He wouldn't say one thing and mean something else, but I suppose it must be difficult for a gambler to play strictly by the rules.'

'One thing is certain, *donna mia*, this between us is going to be played according to the rules. I knew well enough what was in your mind at your sister's wedding, looking so elegant and thinking such murderous thoughts. Don't you care for children?'

'Not yours!' she said stormily. 'How could I want a child

from a man who forced me to—to——'

'Can't you say the words?' he taunted. 'That night in Naples wasn't so terrible, but you'd sooner be chained to a stake and set afire than admit that I made you feel sensations you didn't know were possible. You were brought up believing the Old Victorian adage that a lady says her rosary while the man behaves like a beast. Poor misguided little Julia! I really must take your emotional education in hand.'

'I—I can do without those sort of lessons——'

'Can you, my dear?' He gave a quiet laugh and bending his tall head placed his lips on the smooth curve of her cheek. 'How innocent of you to suppose that you have a choice! Now shall we go inside before my servants decide that we are going to pitch a tent in the forecourt?'

Light was streaming out from the open door at the top of wide stone steps leading up from the forecourt and a figure in a discreet dark suit was waiting there. They mounted the steps, where to Julia's utter consternation Rome swept her up in his arms. 'Here we are, Giovanni,' he said. 'It's an American custom for a bride to be carried over the threshold of her new home.'

This he proceeded to do, while Julia lay tensely in his arms, wanting to struggle out of them but constrained by the presence of his manservant who watched the procedure with intent dark eyes.

'Ah, it's good to be home.' Rome continued to hold Julia while he glanced around the entrance hall, fairly large with a curve to long recessed windows in which were deep sills upholstered in deep red leather. The walls were panelled but a selection of modern paintings made them seem lighter, and there were flowers in large bowls on a pair of onyx tables.

'Welcome home, *signore—signora.*' The manservant

bowed politely. 'We have followed your instructions, *signore,* and I am sure you will find everything to your satisfaction. You had a pleasant journey?'

'It was a good flight, Giovanni, and now we are both in good appetite. I feel sure Cosenza is preparing a fine meal for us—a wedding supper, no less, eh?'

'*Sí, signore.* She has been busy in the kitchen for hours. Cosenza knows your favourite dishes and she has made up her mind that everything will be perfect for you and the *padrona.*'

'Excellent.' Rome smiled and glanced at Julia, who felt foolish in his arms but was too polite to show her feelings in front of a member of his staff. 'My wife is a slim American, but she has the appetite of an Italian girl and will do full justice to the meal. I think we'll have the table set on the *terrazza* as it's a fine night and the moon will have arisen in about another hour. Our apartment has been prepared, Giovanni?'

'To the letter, *signore.* The workmen were here until this morning and all the redecorations have been carried out as you wished. The rooms are looking *che bello.*'

'Then we'll go upstairs. Inform Cosenza that we'll be ready for our dinner in about an hour.'

'*Sí, signore.*' Giovanni turned towards the door. 'I will fetch up the baggage immediately.'

'*Grazie.*' Still making no attempt to set Julia on her feet, Rome began to mount the staircase, which was panelled by gracious wrought-iron at either side of the treads.

'Aren't you afraid you'll over-exert yourself?' Julia enquired coolly.

'The delicious Italian meal we are going to enjoy will soon refuel my energies.' His grey eyes looked down into hers, their lids half-lowered to show a gleam of sultry amusement. 'Any increase in your weight, *mia cara,* is not yet discernible. I wonder if it will be a large child? My mother always said that I weighed heavily, so if you begin in a while to look big we shall know we have a son on the way, eh?'

Julia compressed her lips and made an involuntary movement in his arms, which tightened their hold.

'Don't do that while I'm on the stairs,' he said. 'I could lose my balance.'

'And I could lose——'

'Don't you dare to say it!' They reached the landing and now his eyes cut into her like steel. 'If you do anything to harm that child, Julia, I promise you I shall wring your lovely neck. Our laws in Italy aren't like those in the States. Here the passions relating to the sexes are taken into consideration and I'd be justified in strangling you if you deliberately tried to have a miscarriage. If you have that in mind, then know my mind as well.'

'An unhappy marriage can make a woman miscarry——' Julia clenched his shoulder with her hand. 'Please put me down. It's one thing to pretend in front of your staff that we're madly in love, but it's unnecessary when we're by ourselves.'

'What I intend with you, Julia, when we're by ourselves, would not be suitable viewing for my staff.' With an abrupt laugh he paused in front of a pair of high oval-shaped doors, a single arm strong and firm around her as he turned the handle and pushed the doors open with his shoulder. He carried her across the room, furnished for sitting in, and opened another set of doors.

The room was high-ceilinged, its walls papered silver-grey, with a design of huge white lilies with golden centres. The wall-lights Rome had flicked on revealed jade-green drapes at the windows that swept with a glamorous fullness to the silvery-grey carpet that covered every inch of the floor. Walking silent and lithe, Rome made for the canopied double bed that was the central focus of the room and there he lowered Julia and leaned over her, his arms supported at either side of her on the silvery silk counterpane.

'Well, Signora Demario, what do you think of your new home? This apartment has been smartened up just for your benefit.'

Unbearably aware of his closeness and the quizzical smile on his lean handsome face, Julia glanced obligingly around the big bedroom. 'It looks like something out of a Joan Crawford movie,' she said in her coolest, most deflating tone of voice.

'You little shrew,' he said softly, and suddenly she was gathered right against him and before she could turn her face away he had captured her lips and pushing her back on the bed he kissed her until she felt as if her breath would stop. It was a kiss ot total possessiveness, crushing her beneath him, reviving for her vivid memories of the strength in his well-kept body. With a gasp rising in her throat she had to open her lips to his in order to breathe, and as the intimacy of his kiss increased she felt a strange helplessness in her limbs, a sense of langour as if his sensuous mouth was absorbing her.

When he let her go she lay there weakly, her lips apart, her eyes partly closed. He unbuttoned her coat and she felt his hand on her waist. 'You're mine, Julia, and you might as well accept it. You have my child in you, and that makes you part of me whether you like it or not.'

'I—I don't like it——' Even her voice had grown weak.

'Then learn to like it, my dear.' He rose to his feet, a hand thrusting at his black hair as he stood tall at the bedside. 'I have my own dressing-room and sauna, so you may have the use of the bathroom, only don't take all night trying to scrub the feel of my hands from your body. My touch is not so repugnant to your silky skin as you like to believe, and I'll teach you before long, my lady, to be a real woman.'

'Haven't you done that already?' Julia sat up, a hand at her disarrayed hair. 'I wouldn't be here in your damned house if you hadn't proved your virility!'

He gave a soft, brief laugh as he strolled towards a door at the far end of the room. 'There are signs, Julia, that you could be quite a woman if you were to let down your hair.'

'I don't have to let down my hair, Rome. You're good at making a woman look as if she's been dragged through a bush.'

'Don't let it worry you, *carina*.' He cast her a taunting look over his shoulder. 'The dishevelled look suits you here in the bedroom, though I like to see you at your most soignée when we dine together. Make yourself lovely for our meal on the *terrazza*, eh? This is our real wedding night; you can't count the one we spent travelling. I never could get into a romantic mood on a jet.'

'Have you brought many women to this house, Rome?' Julia made her way to the dressing-table, trying not to notice that her legs still felt oddly tremulous. She took up a hand mirror that lay there and noticed that it was rather beautiful.

'Only my mother—and you,' he replied. 'That mirror is a genuine Medici, but I bought it for a song in a little shop at Capua. I had it cleaned at a jewellers and it was there I was told its real value. I'm quite good at picking up bargains.'

'Bully for you, *signore*.' She turned the mirror about in her hands and saw the gems encrusted in the frame, which was golden. 'Do you regard me as a bargain as I happen to be a Van Holden?'

'Yes,' he drawled, 'when you come to think of it I did get you for a fairly moderate price. Some people lose a great deal more at my casino than your sister did.'

Julia swung to face him, hardening her green eyes. 'If they have to repay you as I did, Rome, then it's a wonder you haven't other children to show for your resourceful way of collecting your debts! I really know very little about you when you come to think of it.'

'You'll soon know a lot, my dear, but you'd better learn to control your tongue if you don't want to get acquainted with my Italian temper.'

'Do you lose it, Rome, when people get curious about your background? After all, you've admitted to being friends with a Mafia leader.'

'As I told your friend Wineman, there are two sides to my life, as there are two sides to the lives of a lot of men.' Rome drew open the door of his dressing-room. 'I'll leave you to get ready for dinner. Wear something attractive for our wedding eve.'

'Is that an order, *signore*?'

'Merely a request, *carina*. I don't regard you as a member of my staff, so don't pretend to yourself that I do. You're my wife—my bride.'

'Your—pregnant bride, Rome. Hardly romantic!'

'I find it—erotic,' he said, and closed the dressing-room door behind him, leaving her with the filigreed mirror clenched in her hands. Erotic, stimulating to his Latin sensuality, that her body was ripening with his baby. Julia lifted the hand mirror and met her own tormented eyes. Always she had been the big sister who looked after her little sister, and now because of it she was burdened with a marriage she didn't want while Verna enjoyed life with a husband she loved.

Julia's lips had a bitter little twist to them, and she felt their tenderness from the hard pressure of Rome's mouth. There was no love in what he felt for her ... in all its aspects it was profane, even a little brutal when he made her kiss him in that way the girls at charm school had said would give a girl a baby. She ran the top of her tongue around the velvety innerside of her lips and reproduced slightly the sensations he had caused. A shiver ran through her body. Oh God, why couldn't she be married to Paul? He had been so kind and courtly. He wouldn't dream of treating her the way Rome did ... Rome was such a boundless, arrogant brute, with none of the sensitive qualities she liked in a man. He was like some untamed animal, graceful to look at but with the instincts of the lower East Side where he had grown up, adept with his fists, part of a tough gang of boys, who had wooed and won girls in the dark alleys at the back of the dance halls where the music had a heavy sensual beat to it.

That she was Julia Van Holden who had led a sheltered life meant nothing to him. He was out to prove to her that as far as he was concerned she was just a girl who ought to be grateful he had done the honourable thing and married her. It was, for him, the most subtle form of revenge he could take on her family, whom he despised as snobs who had no feelings of pity or understanding for those who had to live in poverty. Julia suspected this might have been true of her grandmother, but it wasn't true of her. She could be compassionate, but the man she was married to had long outgrown the need for compassion.

She gazed around the bedroom with its silvery and jade tones ... a new, strange, unlooked-for world which she must come to terms with; to touch and feel and somehow accept. She had been sarcastic about the room, but there were signs of good taste in all its aspects. Colours and furnishings in no way clashed, and irresistibly her gaze was drawn to the bed where the silk cover was still disarranged from her tussle there with Rome.

Defiance and consternation swept through Julia, and she thought again what a naïve idiot she had been to actually believe that a man with Rome's temperament would bring a wife to his home and then treat her as if she were his ward.

She looked at the Medici mirror in her hand and felt an urge to smash it, but instead with a sigh she replaced it on the dressing-table, where there were little porcelain boxes in various sizes, with charming patterns of flowers and peacocks. Over by one of the windows stood a peacock-back chair in ivory canework and on a small table nearby a lovely figured clock in porcelain. Against a wall was the towering shape of a wardrobe in ivory wood and on impulse she went and opened its doors. She stood there stunned, for on rows of hangers were dresses and suits of various lengths, for daytime and evening wear. On a rack there was a selection of lovely Italian shoes, and on another a line of matching handbags. There were gloves, silk scarves, and a vanity case with diamond initials.

Feeling sure she had stumbled on the wardrobe of a girl-friend of Rome's, Julia was far less certain when she saw that the initials were JCD, standing for Julia Caroline Demario!

She swallowed a dryness from her throat and bent down to open a long white box that lay under the dresses. Swathed in sheets of tissue paper was a black diamond mink wrap, soft, shining and incredibly expensive. An envelope jutted from a sleeve and out of pure curiosity Julia opened it and drew out the card inside. Rome had written on it: 'I found out that while you were in Naples you visited the Tonio Gulli fashion house. As they had your measurements it wasn't difficult to get you kitted out with these garments.

You'll wear them, of course.'

With a flash of temper she ripped the card into pieces. It was typical of Rome to assume that like his other women she'd be thrilled to be given the dresses and the mink wrap —like someone he was keeping who had to be kept sweet with presents!

Julia slammed shut the wardrobe doors and when she swung round there was a rap on the bedroom door and Giovanni entered with the baggage. The larger case of pigskin was Rome's and the manservant took it to him. Julia was standing there as if she wanted to pick up her own cases and make a dash from the house when someone else came into the bedroom. The woman was wearing a discreet beige-coloured dress with a lacy cap pinned to her hair, and it was her hair that caught Julia's attention, a flamboyant ginger at which Grandma Van Holden had always frowned, though Lucie Jennings had been too good a nursemaid to be dismissed because of her hair.

'Lucie?' Julia could hardly believe her eyes ... it seemed incredible to see right now someone from out of the past whom she had last seen when she was fifteen, when Lucie had left Grandma's employ to marry a ship's steward. Julia approached her and caught hold of her hands, as if only touch would make her real.

'My dear Lucie, what are you doing here? In Italy of all places ... in this house?'

'Your husband hired me, Miss Julia.' Lucie still had the sprightly voice that matched her hair. 'He found out where I was working in New York and he——'

'But you're married, Lucie!'

'I'm a widow, miss.' Lucie looked sombre for a moment. 'My Bert died when the *Maria Ives* went down. You must have read it in the papers? There was a collision with one of them oil tankers and only a few passengers and crew survived. It happened eighteen months ago.'

'I'm so sorry, Lucie. I had no idea your husband was on that ship.'

'There you are, miss, what is to be will be, as the saying goes. I returned to my old line of work, and then when this offer came from out of the blue—well, I couldn't turn down the chance to take care of you again. My Miss Julia, the nicest lady I ever had in my charge. I must say I was surprised, you being married to Signor Demario. I recall his poor mother, such a nice woman but always on the sad side. It must have been hard on him, being just a boy at the time she worked for your grandma. A real tartar she was! I read in the papers she'd passed away—she was always good to you and Miss Verna, I'll say that for her. Perhaps a bit too fussy and protective, but you were a pretty pair and your parents were dead and I suppose it was understandable.'

Lucie gazed at Julia as the old memories swept over both of them, and then the ginger hair gave that electrical crackle as Lucie shook her head from side to side. 'I wonder what your grandma would say about your marriage, miss? To think of you—and him! Mrs Demario's boy all grown up into such a fine handsome man!'

'He was always good-looking.' A tremor ran through Julia; not even to kind-hearted Lucie could she confide the truth behind her marriage. 'I wonder what made him think of hiring you, Lucie?'

'I reckon he remembered what good friends we were when you were a girl. He seems a very resourceful man, and when he said I'd be looking after you again! Why, it seems only yesterday that I was brushing your long smooth hair in the nursery at your grandma's house. Such hair, and it's still as bright and shining. Cook used to say you owed it to your Dutch ancestors.'

'I expect I do.' Julia smiled slightly, remembering the portrait of Henryk Van Holden which used to fascinate her when she was a child; big, blond, with a pirate's patch over his left eye. He had founded the family fortune, but now all the money was gone and the big old house on Brookside was a tenement.

Julia's smile faded and she gave a sigh. 'Life moves on in mysterious ways, doesn't it, Lucie? Do you believe some things happen because fate means them to?'

'I haven't much doubt of it, miss. Look at the way you and the *signore* have come together again—why, he must've been about eleven years old the last time I saw him. You liked him then, didn't you?'

'Liked—him?' Julia exclaimed. 'What makes you say that? He never used to speak to me, but he often scowled!'

Lucie gave a laugh. 'Boys are sometimes like that when they have an eye on a girl. You were the princess in the castle and he must've made up his mind all that time ago to marry you.'

'No.' Julia shook her head emphatically. 'He never intended to marry me—that's just the way it turned out. I must say you're looking well, Lucie, and your hair still has that lovely crackling sound Verna and I used to love to hear when we got you rattled. You know that Verna's married as well?'

'Yes, you know what a one I am for reading the gossip columns. You've both done well for yourselves, haven't you?' Lucie gazed around the big silvery bedroom. 'Isn't this glamorous? Those long sweeping curtains, that enormous bed, and a carpet you can sink into up to your ankles. I bet Mrs Demario must be proud of the way her boy has got on in the world?'

'She died,' Julia said quietly. 'My husband isn't in business, he runs a gambling casino in Naples. I suppose you could say that he's very successful at that sort of thing.'

Lucie frowned slightly as she studied Julia. 'I wasn't sure what he did for a living. Giovanni speaks English, but he isn't the sort to tell you much, and his wife is all Italian like those pizzas she makes. The daughter is a flighty one, with an eye for the men, so I can't say I have much to do with her. The name they've given her—Maddalena! If you ask me, she'll be living up to it!'

'She works here in the house?' Julia asked.

'If you can call flicking a duster round the rooms her main occupation,' Lucie said tartly. 'She spends half the day hanging around the gardener, who isn't all wrinkled and taciturn like old Jeffers who used to take care of your grandma's garden. This one goes around bare to the waist, with a gold chain around his neck and a tattoo of a pierced heart on his arm. He knows his job, but all the same he looks as if he belongs in a dance hall.'

Julia smiled. 'Something of a Valentino, eh?'

Lucie nodded, her gaze fixed upon Julia's face. 'You've lost that little-girl look I remember, Miss Julia, as if everything had a kind of wonderment. The bones in your face stand out in a lovely way, and you're so grown-up and elegant, but there's something—maybe a bit of grief still for your grandma.'

'Yes,' Julia agreed quickly, 'I do miss her. Verna and I were with her such a long time.'

Lucie nodded. 'It's only to be expected that you miss her, especially now you're a newlywed and would like her advice and approval.'

'Do you honestly think she'd approve?' Suddenly Julia was laughing, but it was the kind of laughter on the edge of tears and she didn't dare to enjoy the self-pity which might lead to her confiding in Lucie. She had to remember that Lucie was employed by Rome and she, as his wife, owed him loyalty even if she didn't love him.

'I'd better get a move on.' She swallowed the painful lump in her throat. 'Rome and I are dining in less than an hour and I guess he'll be annoyed if I spoil the meal by keeping him waiting. Oh, what shall I wear? There isn't time to unpack my case—Lucie, he's gone and crammed that wardrobe with clothes, so will you select a dress for me while I take a shower?'

Ten minutes later she came out of the bathroom, onyx-tiled with a sunken tub, its pedestal basin, double-u and bidet in a water-lily pattern. Lucie had selected *eau-de-nil* undergarments to go with a long velvet dress in deep jade green, the charming simplicity of the style accentuated by a slim jewelled belt, the neckline softly rounded to show off Julia's creamy skin.

Julia touched the velvet dress and hesitated. 'Perhaps something less dressy,' she murmured. 'It isn't as though we're having guests——'

'Mr Rome chose the dress, miss.' Lucie picked it up and held it ready for Julia to step into. 'He came in a few minutes ago and took it off the wardrobe hanger himself. You'll want to please him—won't you?'

Words of denial trembled on Julia's lips, and then with a slight shrug she allowed Lucie to assist her into the dress, which she had to admit fitted her perfectly. The skirt shimmered like the green colour in a peacock's fantail and Julia's fingertips stroked it as Lucie clasped the belt about her waist. How long would it be, Julia wondered, before it really began to show that she was carrying a child? So far there was only a minimal alternation in her contours, adding just a slight fullness to her hips and breast, and when she turned to the mirror she had to admit to herself that the dress was attractive on her . . . adding a slight voluptuousness Rome would notice at once.

'Oh, you do look a picture, miss!' Lucie exclaimed. 'The *signore* certainly knows what suits you, and they say that's the sign of a really attentive man.'

Julia's heart gave a disturbing throb. She had pleaded for Rome's inattentiveness, but she could see for herself that he would approve of her in the dress of his choice, which seemed to compliment the smooth creaminess of her skin and the ashen shine of her hair.

Lucie went to the dressing-table, for Julia stood in front of a full-length mirror whose long oval frame was a moulding of gilded birds and imps. Through the mirror Julia saw Lucie open a small case and take from it something that gleamed in her fingers.

'Mr Rome said you must wear this with the dress, miss. Isn't it charming?'

Julia turned to Lucie, who was holding a necklace so it caught the light of the lamps. Strung on stems of gold were buds and flowers made of emeralds with diamond centres, and even as the female in Julia responded to the charm of the necklace, she resented passionately the way her husband was wooing her with expensive gifts . . . letting her know with each presentation that she was going to give him in return the pleasure of her body.

She took a deep shaking breath, as if something constricted her heart. In every way he had bought her . . . first with the money Verna had lost to him, then with a wedding ring that saved her from indignity, and now with costly dresses and jewels. She had called herself his toy, and as if wound up with a little key that made her respond, she allowed Lucie to place the necklace around her neck and clasp its diamond catch.

'You look lovely, Miss Julia.' Lucie smoothed the dress and the fair hair, which lay in a soft upcurl on the velvet. Julia wore very little make-up, and her mouth had a vulnerable curve to it. 'Everyone used to say your sister was prettier, but I always knew you'd grow up to be the elegant one. My, you should have your portrait painted just as you are! I wonder if the *signore* will think the same?'

'I don't imagine so.' Rome, in Julia's cynical estimation, wanted a woman he could touch, not a painting of her to look at. He wasn't an artistic sort of man like Paul Wineman who appreciated elegance for its own sake, not as something he wanted to disorder with his hands, uncaring if nylon laddered, if silk ripped and soft skin bruised in an effort to escape the lips that stole a woman's right to surrender herself with love.

Julia met Lucie's eyes and saw in them a kind of puzzlement, as if she was beginning to notice the lack of warmth and eagerness in Julia's attitude towards the man she had married.

'I—I was always the reserved one, remember?' Julia applied a little perfume to her neck and wrists. 'In several ways Verna and I are unalike—I guess you could say she's the ardent one.'

'Still waters run deep, miss.' Lucie gave Julia a careful scrutiny. 'It's in deep waters where the best fishing is supposed to be, and some men like it that way, so I've heard.'

'You and your sayings,' Julia smiled. 'I am glad you're here, Lucie, to take care of me. Now the house doesn't feel quite so alien.'

'My Bert always said I had a cheerful face. Now you go and have a nice dinner with the *signore*, out there on the *terrazza* in the moonlight. My, but he has grown up to be handsome! Gives even a middle-aged body like me a kick to look at that face of his, not to mention his fine figure. He's straight as the Guardsmen at the Palace.'

'Do you miss London?' Julia asked. 'Didn't you want to go back there when you lost your husband?'

'Not really, miss. I've worked too many years in America, and now this is quite a change for me, working in Italy. It's lovely and warm in this part of the country—there's something romantic about it.'

'I always thought you had a romantic soul.' Julia's gaze settled on the bed that dominated the bedroom and she felt a tremor deep down inside her. There seemed so little romance in her marriage ... she was here because she had no choice, and it wouldn't be too long before Lucie realised that she was going to have Rome's baby and that it had been conceived some weeks before their marriage.

Resentment stirred again through Julia's body. She had been her own private person until fate had thrown her into Rome's ruthless arms ... those arms which the Italian sun had tanned to a deep gold. His skin all over was a golden hue, holding in it a sensual warmth that Julia remembered, and ran from the bedroom in an effort to forget.

CHAPTER FOUR

JULIA stood poised at the head of the stairs, gazing down the long sweep of them to the hall. In a romantic novel she had read at charm school the heroine had fallen down a flight of stairs and lost her baby . . . she had wanted it and the husband had been the one who didn't care. Julia put out a hand and gripped the stair rail. It was crazy to compare real life with fiction, and much as she wanted to be free of Rome she didn't fancy a broken neck in the process.

One hand on the rail and the other holding the long skirt of her dress Julia descended the stairs with the unaware grace she had possessed even as a child. She had a natural air of composure which had always masked her hurts and bruises, and the only time she had cried in front of others had been at Verna's party . . . the memory was still so vivid, of a boy uninvited to join in the fun and games because he was the cleaning woman's son. Proud and fierce, he had flung her offering of ice-cream at her feet and when it splashed her shoes and white socks she had burst into tears. Maybe that was why her grandmother had been that extra bit angry, seeing her in tears when she so rarely gave way to them.

Lost in her thoughts, Julia arrived at the foot of the stairs to find the object of her memories waiting there, and as always it was confusing to find the intense boy lost in the tall worldly man. Her eyes locked startled with his as she stood poised on the final step to the hall. His lean face was shaven except for the darkness of his sideburns and she felt deep inside her a movement, a spasm, as if within the womb his child reached out to him.

It was unsettling and as if he sensed this Rome reached out and took hold if her hand. As he did so his eyes moved up and down her figure in the velvet dress.

'You,' he murmured, 'are a lovely thing to see.'

'So you've already informed me,' she said coolly.

'Not in so many words, my dear.'

'Your eyes do the speaking for you—they always did.'

'I'm a grown up man now, Julia. If you gave me ice-cream now I wouldn't throw it back at you.'

A warmth ran over her skin, for he gave the words a sensual meaning; her fingers tensed within his, but she only managed to pull her gaze from his. His dinner jacket was a deep aubergine colour, superbly tailored to his lean hard figure. Julia noticed the fine quality silk of his shirt and tie, the way his tapered trousers fitted without a crease. He was straight like a Guardsman, but with a supple, animal ease that Julia felt in him as he tucked her hand into the crook of his arm and walked her across the hall and out upon the wide *terrazza* at the rear of the villa.

It overhung the sea like the prow of a galleon, and was balustraded by a fretwork of iron. A circular table was set with fine china and silver on lace and so still was the night that candles had been lit in silver sticks. There were big terracotta pots against the parapet wall, in which flowers of various sorts spilled over the sides. Lanterns shone here and there on the terrace and shadows lit mysteriously a few remnants of Roman statuary.

Over all hung the scent of the sea, and overhead the moon was awesomely full, like a great golden pendant attached to a string of diamonds, the stars that paled to obscurity beside that glowing orb.

'What a night!' Rome exclaimed. 'Do you know that line

of Browning's, "Open my heart and you will see graved inside of it, Italy"?'

'I can see that America could never hold you,' Julia replied. 'You're an Italian in every cell of your body, aren't you? Looks, instincts, roots! You belong here, but I don't.'

'A woman learns to adapt, Julia. Women are good at that because their roots can re-establish themselves in the man rather than the land.'

'That remark is so arrogantly male,' she rejoined. 'As if without a man a woman is rootless.'

'Most women are, my dear.'

'And what do you call a man without a woman?'

'A damned fool.' Rome's grey eyes were moonlit, and amused as they met hers. 'There isn't any part of a man that doesn't get pleasure from the woman he wants to be with. All his senses are involved ... what he sees, touches, breathes, hears and speaks to. A woman pleasures the possessive instinct in a man.'

'And yours is particularly potent, isn't it, Rome?' She slid into the chair and was very aware of him standing over her, her spine tensing as she felt his hand slide over her hair.

'Yes, I like the feeling of being the owner of fine things,' he agreed. 'I like it very much that you have elegance and class, like this Versalini goblet.'

He picked up the goblet, which had graceful patterns in the glass and was set on a shining stem. He moved it about in his fingers by the stem and there was a faint smile on his lips, and then abruptly his eyes met Julia's as he struck a fingernail against the crystal and it made a ringing sound. 'Aren't you going to thank me for the surprise you found upstairs?'

Julia touched the necklace. 'It's very nice, thank you,' she said politely.

His fingers tightened on the stem of the wine glass and she stared fascinated, for his fingers were strong enough to snap it. 'By God, Julia, I could take you by the neck when you put on that milady air of yours and don't really care a damn if I gave you nothing. Other women——'

'Yes,' she broke in, 'what would other women do? Lick your shoes?'

'Not my shoes, Julia.'

She flushed and had an image of another woman in his arms, held milky-pale and yielding against the tawny gold skin, her lips moving in sensuous kisses over his body. There was no doubt in Julia's mind that what she imagined had often been a reality. The warmth in Rome's skin went deep into his flesh and bone and he would always have needed the touch of a woman. She remembered how his mother used to look when she brushed the tousled black hair out of his eyes after he came back from running an errand, or had been helping old Jeffers in the garden. There had been pride and love and a hint of fear in Mrs Demario's eyes, as if she had known that the force of life would be powerful in her son as he grew up to be a man and there would be no way she could keep him safe from women and danger.

Both had been attracted to Rome, and Julia knew it as she watched him replace the lovely wine glass on the lace tablecloth.

'I wasn't thinking of the necklace,' he drawled.

Julia caught her breath as comprehension struck her. 'You mean Lucie?'

'Of course I mean Lucie.' He strolled round to his own chair, beside which stood a stand with a silver bucket holding a bottle of wine. He withdrew the bottle from the ice and took a look at the label, nodded his satisfaction and sat down. 'Are you pleased with her, at least?'

'Oh yes.' This time there was fervency in Julia's voice. 'I was so surprised to see her after all this time—what made you think of asking her to come to Italy?'

'I thought you would like with you someone you had known as a child and trusted.' He caught and held Julia's gaze across the table. 'I know it isn't easy for a girl when she's having her first baby. You will have need of the good Lucie. She's kind and sensible and she knows your little ways better than anyone. She was probably more of a mother to you than your tartar of a grandparent, who always looked as if she was locked body and feelings into whalebone.'

'Grandma was good to Verna and me. It was a great shock to her when our parents were killed on that safari during the Kenya uprising. It wasn't until I grew older that I learned about the Mau-Mau and what they did to white people who fell into their hands.'

'I know.' His face went sombre. 'Put it out of your mind, *carina.* Don't be haunted by it.'

'In case I damage your child, Rome? I've heard that one about beautiful thoughts making beautiful babies, so I'll think about that night in Naples instead.'

'Santo Dio!' He banged a hand down on the table and shook the china and stemware, and made the candle flames quake in the silver sticks. 'Can't we ever enjoy a meal without a mention of Naples, and what you like to think of as my animal lust?'

'It's why I'm here,' she retorted. 'I don't happen to prefer a dinner *à deux* with you to being with friends of my own choosing, whose company I find congenial.'

'You no doubt have the aesthetic and courtly Paul Wineman on your mind.' Rome raised his left eyebrow in a sardonic way. 'I'll permit him to be there, but elsewhere is my province. Quite frankly, I couldn't imagine that he'd know what to do with a woman if he ran out of artistic conversation.'

'Don't judge Paul by your standards,' she rejoined. 'Machismo isn't everything in a man—some women find it a bit of a bore.'

'Not those I've known, *donna mia.*'

'Dance hall girls and silly women who bet on bad numbers?'

'By the saints——' Abruptly he laughed. 'They should have named you Kate, not the sweeter name of Julia, which sounds like Juliet.'

'Romeo and Juliet!' It was her turn to laugh. 'They should have named you Tarquin!'

The amusement fled his eyes and suddenly they were like hot steel in his dark face. 'I didn't pounce on you in the dark, my dear. You asked for a levelling when you called me lowdown. I don't take that kind of talk from anyone, least of all from a Van Holden. Didn't you realise, you little fool, that you had those IOUs almost in the palm of your hand? I was going to give them to you after I'd made you plead a little, but you had to let me know how superior you thought yourself. Superiority has no defence against nature, has it, Julia? It got the better of both of us for I'm usually in better control of that kind of situation.'

'Meaning?' She flung up her chin as she looked across at him.

'Meaning, my dear, that I don't usually get the girl into trouble. You must have gone to my head.'

'Your head, Rome?'

He stared at her and she heard the catch of his breath. 'Watch out, Julia, or you might become human.'

'It's because I'm darned well human that I'm stuck with you!' She forced her gaze from his and glanced over to where those remnants of statuary caught the moonlight on their pale stonework. 'I—I hate bits and pieces of stone torsos, but you Latins seem to find them fascinating.'

'Mainly because sculpture was quite an art in Italy and Greece.' He broke a breadstick and crunched it. 'Michelangelo thought the male body one of the supreme creations, but I take the opposite view. The touch of a woman by soft lamplight is comparable only to perfect pizza and hot melting cheese—ah, and here comes Giovanni with some of that good Italian food! *Che bello!* It smells good!'

Julia felt her own hungry response to the appetising *pasta e fagioli* which was served to them in earthenware bowls, a soup crammed with chopped vegetables and spaghetti, thick, spicy and hot. Chunks of home-baked bread were placed on the table and the chilled wine was poured into the Versalini glasses.

'I know what you're thinking.' Rome gave her an amused look. 'Posh wine glasses with peasant soup bowls, eh? Maybe it's a combination which typifies the Italian, combining his lusty appetite with his eye for beauty. Go to the opera at La Scalá and you will see Italians as enthralled by *Tosca* as by the salami in their sandwiches.'

'Italian opera is very schmaltzy,' she said.

'So is *Tristan und Isolde*, and the *Liebestod.*'

'Do you go often?'

'Occasionally to the San Carlo, if I'm in a romantic mood.' He raised his wine glass and studied the wine through the patterns in the crystal. 'This is called a Lacrima Cristi, the tears of Christ, and the grapes for it are grown on the slopes of Vesuvius. You have to admit, Julia, that we Italians have a flair for drama.'

'I'd be the last to deny it.' She took a sip of the wine, which had a creamy, slightly biting sweetness. 'Not that I've ever known many.'

'Then knowing me will be quite an education for you,

mia.' He broke bread and bit into it with his firm white teeth.

'You lived in the States all those years,' she said wonderingly, 'and yet no one would take you for anything but an Italian. You've reverted to type absolutely and could have been born here rather than there.'

'We invariably spoke Italian and ate this kind of food. I attended Mass each Sunday with my mother—not that I pretend to be religious in the sense that I abide by all the rules of our church. Maybe I enjoyed the ritual.'

'You must surely believe in hellfire and damnation,' she murmured.

He narrowed his eyes at her and the candle flames made a frame of shadows about the boldness of his face. 'Meaning?'

'Well, you aren't exactly sinless, are you, Rome? Unless, of course, you go to confession.'

'I do go, on occasion.'

'When you're feeling in a guilty mood?'

He made no reply but just looked at her across the candlelit table, while in the silvered garden the *cigales* chirred in the cypress and ilex, and the blue trees as he had called them.

'You're a pagan,' she said. 'You feel no guilt about me, do you?'

'None,' he agreed shamelessly. 'I'd have hated my own guts had I left you to go and have an instrument used on your body. There are men who do that, but I have a sense of responsibility. Grant me that at least, *donna mia.*'

'You have a sense of ownership,' she retorted. 'Tell me, Rome, what makes you so sure I'm having *your* baby?'

'Of course it's mine!'

'Can any man say that with total certainty?'

'I can say it because I know you, Julia.'

'You knew me as a child, but we met in Naples as adults.'

'I was adult,' he tipped wine into his mouth, 'but you were just a more grown-up version of the little girl. You were quite innocent.'

'Yes, until I met you I was innocent,' she agreed. 'When I returned to New York I was a different person—and Paul was there.'

Rome laid down his soup spoon very carefully and she saw the candle flames reflected in his grey eyes, intensifying their dangerous beauty. His lashes and eyebrows looked night-dark in contrast, and Julia felt the heavy beating of her heart as he raked those eyes over her face, her neck, down over the velvet-covered curve of her breast.

'The child is mine,' he grated. 'That effete friend of yours could only get excited over a Monet water-lily—if he found a woman in his arms he wouldn't know what to do with her. He'd probably start to lecture on Byzantine fruit bowls!'

'Oh, very amusing, Rome. Will you laugh when the baby arrives with blond hair, I wonder?'

'Stop this nonsense, Julia.' His voice had developed an edge. 'I've only to touch you to know I'm the man who's made you pregnant. If I took you in my arms right now I'd feel that instinctive response of your flesh—oh yes, my dear, it happens and I feel it, whether you like it or not. It's a bond you can't easily snap with your lying little teeth. Part of me is there inside you, so stop pretending you ever slept with any man but me!'

'You're getting quite het up, Rome.' Julia moved her fingers up and down the stem of her wine glass and inside her she felt the pleasure of teasing him; of perhaps shaking him out of his self-confidence. 'You aren't really all that certain, are you? You know American girls are more liberated than Italians because you lived in the States where you danced with them and dated them. The only thing Italian about me is your name——'

'This has gone far enough!' He leaned across the table angrily and in so doing knocked one of the lighted candles out of the socket of its silver stick. The candle fell in Julia's direction and the flame caught the lace cloth and ran towards the opening of her sleeve, not actually touching her but causing her to give a cry of fear. Instantly Rome had snatched up the water jug and flung the contents over the flames and unavoidably into Julia's lap. She felt the wetness soaking through the velvet as she scrambled out of her chair and stood shaking her skirt.

The dining-table was now a shambles and as Rome thrust away from it one of the Versalini goblets fell to the ground and there was a sound of shattered glass.

'*Santo Dio*, are you all right?' He didn't even glance at the breakage but caught hold of Julia's arm, raising it so he could examine her skin.

'I'm wet,' she rejoined. 'Ugh, nothing feels quite so awful as wet velvet! And just look at the table!'

Giovanni arrived at that precise moment carrying their second course, and when he saw the state of the table he nearly dropped the tray.

'It's all right,' Rome placated, 'I knocked over a candle and set light to the cloth. I've made something of a mess and the *signora* has to change her clothes. We'll go upstairs, Giovanni. Bring the food and the wine and we'll finish our dinner there.'

'*Si, signore.*' The manservant was doing his utmost to look impassive. 'A wine glass has been broken, one that you valued.'

'My own clumsiness was at fault.' Rome shrugged. 'Stop pulling faces, Julia. You have many changes of dress upstairs.'

'Ugh!' She was trying to hold the heavy wetness of the velvet away from her legs, and with an abrupt laugh Rome lifted her into his arms and carried her from the *terrazza.*

'Damn you!' She punched his shoulder in a flash of temper and a residue of fright. 'Did you have to throw half the water over me? I bet you did it on purpose!'

'I had to act quickly, *cara.* You could have been burned.'

'It was your fault,' she said stormily.

'You were the one who started the contretemps. You set out to annoy me and you know it, Julia.'

Up the stairs he strode with her, carrying her as effortlessly as if she were a small girl instead of a grown woman. In striking his shoulder she had felt the smooth hardness of the muscle, a Latin of innate toughness who had probably learned how to fight at one of the East Side gymnasiums; who could probably swim like a fish and play a hard game of baseball.

In every sort of way their lives had been different, and yet here they were together ... they were man and wife, and the full impact struck at Julia as he lowered her to her feet in the bedroom he had every right to share with her.

She felt the invasive fear and shyness as she looked at him, so big and dark in the silvery bedroom, his black hair disordered on his brow and a slight quirk to his mouth.

'Come, you must change out of this damp dress before you catch a chill.' His fingers touched the clasp of the jewelled belt and she backed away from him.

'I—I can manage, thank you.' Julia waited for him to turn his back, but he obviously had no such intention and with a flushed face and a resentful nervousness she unclasped the belt and sought with a shaky hand the zip fastening at the back of the dress.

'Let me do that.' He came behind her and right down her backbone she was aware of his bigness as he slid open the zip until the velvet loosened around her. He gave it a push and it fell around her ankles and she was vulnerably exposed for his eyes in her satin slip. It was damp as well and would have to come off, and even as she gave a tormented little shiver he pulled the straps off her shoulders so the garment also slid to her feet. Now she stood there in only her bra and panties, feeling the heavy beat of her heart as he deliberately turned her to face him, his hands warm upon the smooth skin of her upper arms.

'I'm your husband,' he said softly. 'You mustn't be shy of me, *cara.* I have the right to see you like this.'

'I—I want my robe.' She tried to pull away from him, but she hadn't a fraction of his strength and could only gasp helplessly when he drew her against him and buried his warm lips against her neck.

'*Come è bella,*' he murmured. 'You can't know how sweet and soft and inviting you are! I want you——'

'No—please!' She struggled in his arms. 'Giovanni will be arriving any minute w-with our dinner——'

'I'm hungry for you, *carissima.* I want to take you to bed —I want the scent of you, the feel of your hair, those throbbing little cries—ah, it was good—you know it was good!'

'It was bad—hateful,' she breathed. 'You made me——'

'Yes, I made you, but tonight will be different. You won't fight me so I have to hurt you, you will relax and let me love your sweet silky—ah, God, don't shake like that, as if I'm some ugly monster who has hold of you!'

'You're ugly to me——'

'*Santo Dio!*' He thrust her away so she stumbled. His eyes blazed in his tense face. 'If I were Naples born I'd slap your face and throw you on that bed. I'd really show you what it's like to be forced—when that happens, my dear, there are no preliminaries but plenty of pain. Do you want that? Will that really give you a reason to hate me?'

'I already have sufficient reason.' She snatched at her robe and struggled into it. 'If I cried out that last time it was because you hurt me.'

'Not that much, my dear Julia. I'm a shade too experienced not to know the difference—that's right, tie that sash in knots and cover up your body or you might let loose the beast again. What's the real matter, Julia, is it me or yourself that you're afraid of?'

She scorned to answer him, and with a shrug he went and sprawled in the peacock-back chair. Julia smoothed her hair as Giovanni tapped on the door.

'I've laid the table in the adjoining room, *signore*.' Giovanni kept his gaze politely averted from Julia in her negligee. 'Cosenza made a pot of coffee in case the *signora* had need of a cup.'

'*Splendido.*' Rome lounged to his feet and cast a lazily insolent look over Julia. 'Cosenza is a woman of feelings—well, my dear, shall we go and proceed with our dinner?'

Julia preceded him into the *salone*, lit by ruby-shaded lamps, the table in front of the lounger laid out with their meal. It all looked very intimate and cosy, but stirred up in Julia feelings that were far from cosy.

'We shan't require any further service tonight, Giovanni.' Rome smiled as he gazed around the *salone*. 'Thank your wife for her efforts on our behalf.'

'You are both more than welcome, *signore*.' Giovanni glanced at Julia. '*Buona notte, signora.*'

'Goodnight,' she said. 'I'm sorry your beautifully arranged table on the *terrazza* was spoiled. I suppose the wine glass was broken beyond repair?'

'*Sí, signora.*' Giovanni spread his hands regretfully. 'Such a pity, but crystal of that quality shatters into fragments if dropped and there is nothing to be done.'

'*Che disastro!*' Rome laughed. 'It's only an object and I

daresay it can be replaced. There are other things of far more value, and I'd smash a dozen Versalinis rather than see an inch of soft skin burned.'

Julia felt the rise of heat under her skin, for his voice dwelt on the words and made her relive the feel of his hands on her body. What was inanimate could never mean as much to Rome as something that was warm and living to his touch, and as she took a seat on the lounger she gathered the flimsy protection of her robe closely around her. The *salone* door closed behind Giovanni and she was alone with her husband, who before sitting down beside her took off his tie and opened the collar of his silk shirt. It was the casual action of a man making himself comfortable in his home, but nothing that Rome did in Julia's presence seemed ordinary. Nothing about Rome Demario was ordinary.

'Shall we have some of that coffee?' Julia felt the give of the lounger as he sat down. 'You can be mother.'

She gave him a withering look as she picked up the pot and filled the cups. He took his scalding dark with a spoonful of brown sugar, but indicated with a flick of his finger that she add cream to hers. Julia was tempted to oppose him, except that she liked her coffee sweet and creamy.

'Ah, this room is really rather charming.' He glanced around him with a gleam of satisfaction in his eyes. 'When I first bought the villa it was much neglected and I didn't bother too much about the upper rooms because my mother couldn't manage the stairs and had her apartment on the ground floor. I'm pleased with the look of these rooms. The colour schemes have worked out well.'

His eyes met Julia's over the rim of his coffee cup. 'Don't you agree?'

'Yes,' she said indifferently. 'You like to think you do everything with style, don't you, *signore*?'

'Don't you think that I do, *carina*?' He gave a brief laugh.

'No, perhaps you don't—I'm the upstart from the East Side who dared to pull you off the pedestal where you were just a charming image of a woman. I made you face the fact that there's more to being a woman than poise and politeness and the sweet charity of your company. Your Park Avenue clique might be satisfied with that kind of companionship, but it won't satisfy me. I don't intend to have a sweet piece of ice for a wife, and you'll melt, Julia, one way or another.'

'Would you like to take a bet on it, Rome?' His self-assurance seemed to curl across her skin like the tip of a lash. 'You're a gambling man, so a bet with such long odds should appeal to you.'

'The odds aren't all that long, my dear.' His smile was taunting. 'There is one formula in this life that no scientist has been able to mix in a test tube, and that's the magnetism that brings a man and woman together. Fight it, deny it, and try to suppress it, but when I touch you, just here on your inner arm, you feel it elsewhere, don't you—just as I do?'

Julia jerked her arm from the insinuation of his hand up the butterfly sleeves of her robe. 'Don't confuse my reactions with those of your numerous girl-friends,' she said coldly.

'I wouldn't dream of doing so. They were never the challenge that you are, *maaonna.* They never had your defiant green eyes and your hair that I know to be naturally that colour and texture, nor your virginal shrinking.' He softly laughed as his eyes moved over her hair and down her figure. 'You have my baby in you, and yet you still manage to look as if you had never been touched.'

'You haven't touched my heart, Rome, so perhaps that's the reason.'

'Always you have an answer, haven't you, Julia?' His lip

quirked as he started to eat his dinner, beautifully cooked pheasant meat and sweet corn, with potatoes which had been perfectly baked. Everything of the best, Julia thought, as she ate the food. A superb cook in his kitchen, a manservant who served him as if he were a scion of the nobility, and a house whose fundamental charm he had gradually restored until it was probably worth three times what he had paid for it.

He was without doubt a shrewd, clever and ruthless man, and it gave her a curiously helpless feeling that she could no longer find in him the boy outside the French windows who watched her dance in her rose-coloured dress and buckled shoes. There was no trace of him in the Roman nose, the lean and darkly defined jaw, deeply clefted at the centre of his chin. Yet that night in Naples she had known who he was from the moment she set eyes on him. She had walked into his casino and their eyes had met beneath the glitter of the chandeliers above the gaming tables and for an instant time had stood still ... briefly, between one heartbeat and another, they had been boy and girl again, that very last time on the terrace of her grandmother's house.

'Come, eat up your dinner,' he said, as she dawdled, lost in her thoughts. 'It's good for you, and remember you have two to feed.'

'I don't forget it for a minute,' she flashed back at him. 'It really gives you a kick, doesn't it, to have humiliated me! When did the vendetta begin, Rome? That day long ago when I felt sorry for the boy on the outside looking in? I was only a child. I didn't know about the snobbery of people and the stupid distinctions they make because someone has a few more dollars in the bank. I was as much a victim of my background as you were of yours, so why use me to revenge yourself on the system? Don't you do enough of that at the casino when you watch the rich losing their dollars at your tables? That's why you run a casino, isn't it? You know you could do other things, that you have the shrewd mentality to make any sort of business a success.'

'Is that what you'd like, Julia, a respectable businessman for a husband?'

'What I'd like is not to have you for a husband at all!'

'Too bad, my dear. Will you have a few more potatoes and a spoonful of corn? You don't need to worry about your figure.'

'You—I could kill you!' Reluctantly she laughed at his impudence, and at the unavoidable fact that daily her appetite seemed to increase and she knew it was due to her pregnancy. 'This darned child of yours is going to be monstrously big, damn you!'

'That's the Julia I know and love,' he mocked, placing crisp baked potatoes on her plate and two large spoonfuls of the glistening corn. 'It's going to be a boy and we shall name him Lorenzo Sebastian after both our fathers. Mmm, sounds quite effective, don't you agree?'

'I may be carrying a huge girl, who will have great flat feet and your nose, Romeo.'

He stared at her a moment and then gave a laugh. 'I like it when you make a joke, *donna mia*.'

'You think I'm joking?' Julia ran her eyes over his handsome face. 'I have Dutch ancestors and my grandmother was a big woman, and it isn't always the case that children resemble their father. What would you do, Rome, if I produced for you a plain pudding of a daughter?'

'Love her,' he said quietly. 'I'm Italian and we care for our children whether they are pretty or plain.'

'That doesn't go for women where you're concerned, does it, Rome? You like them to be decorative, and I—I wish to heaven I'd come to your casino with my hair in a scarf and wearing trousers! You wouldn't have given me a second look!'

'Nor, very likely, would I have given you your sister's IOUs. Don't pretend to be shocked, Julia. You've said often enough that I'm no saint, and the girl who walked into my casino was wearing a chemise dress in a stunning deep pink, the soft flaxen curve of her hair was held to one side in a silver clip, and her mouth was a velvety red. As I've said, Julia, those IOUs were yours for the taking, but when you opened those soft lips you said some hard things and you made me mad. All I wanted then was to teach you a lesson you wouldn't forget in a hurry.'

'You certainly made sure I wouldn't forget it!' Julia flushed as she remembered the details of that lesson, the way he had driven her backwards to where his bed stood in the shadows of that room above the casino, his eyes brilliant with intent every inch of the way. 'You'll remember this night all your days,' he had promised. 'I'll show you that underneath the fine disdain, my lady, you are just another woman.'

Julia pressed a table napkin to her lips to conceal their tremor. Lithe, tigerish, darkly graceful, he had tracked her to the bed and when he touched her it was as if an electrical current entered her body and made her legs buckle beneath her. She had never known in her life such a panic of heart and nerves, alone for the first time in her life with the kind of man who obeyed no rules where women were concerned. 'You're a no-good worthless brute,' she had raged, 'and I hate every detestable inch of you!'

'You look lovely when you hate a man,' he had mocked. 'Now don't fight me too much or I shall do damage to this charming dress. Remember, you have to go home in it in the morning.'

Julia had to submit to its removal, knowing that if he tore her dress it would be evident to Verna that it had been done at the casino. Her torment had been like that of a trapped animal and she'd stood shivering as the cool air from an open window drifted on to her bare shoulders, until all at once the coolness was replaced by the warmth of a mouth searching the hollows of her neck.

'You infinite devil of a man!' She had punched his chest and tried her hardest to get her knee into him, but he had been too adroit and far too strong, and there had been no escape from him.

It all came rushing back as she met Rome's eyes, the way she noticed in the morning that his skin had a golden sheen to it and that unlike a lot of modern men he didn't wear a gold chain with the inevitable saintly medal buried in his chest hair.

'Can I go now?' she had asked.

'Of course,' he said, handing her the gambling slips. 'Don't forget these—or me.'

'That's the first thing I intend to do when I walk out of this place—forget you!' she had rejoined. He had laughed at her, a molten ripple to his body in the morning sunlight. He had laughed as if he knew that before very long she would have cause to remember him.

'You haven't a bone of remorse in your body, have you, Rome?' Julia studied him in the lamplight of the *salone*. 'You're a predator—you take. I expect in a former life you were a *condottiere*.'

'A soldier of fortune, eh? Not one of the Borgias?' He broke open a purplish fig and carried the sweet inner fruit to his mouth, something very sensual about the action, his eyes fixed lazily upon her face as his white teeth bit into the fruit. 'You know what they say about figs, don't you, *carina*?'

'Yes, you don't have to spell it out!'

'Why not?' He quirked an eyebrow and looked amused. 'Life for you in Blanche Van Holden's house was more than a little repressive, wasn't it, Julia? I don't believe you're naturally a prig, but you were certainly brought up to be one; trained to the eyebrows to become the wife of some anaemic, starch-shirted prig with Wall Street connections. One day you'll thank me for saving you from such a fate.'

'I consider, Rome, that I have very little to thank you for. I was content with my life before you disrupted it, and you might as well know here and now that I intend to continue with that style of life when—all this is over and done with.' She swept her hand down her body, indicating with the gesture that she referred to the child she was carrying. 'You can't hold me, Rome. You can't force me to remain with you. We aren't living in the Middle Ages when even the law didn't care very much what happened to women. I married you for the sake of the child—you swore you married me for the same reason. We aren't in love with each other, and despite what you think of me and my upbringing I want to know what it feels like to be with someone I love.'

'Someone like Wineman?' he taunted. 'I'd have a bit more respect for him if he'd swung a punch at me when I told him you were marrying me, but he stood there like a stick and made no effort at all to fight for you. I wonder what he'd have done had he caught me in his apartment stealing one of his works of art?'

'Men of sensitivity don't show their feelings in your sort of way,' she retorted. 'It might be natural for you to swing a punch at someone who took your girl, but Paul isn't like that. I knew he was upset. I could see it in his eyes.'

'Then you must have terrific vision,' Rome scoffed. 'He was affronted by the obvious fact that I'm Italian, and I know how his sort refer to Latin Americans. We're gigolos, waiters, or racketeers. You talk so primly about going back to your old life when you've had the baby, but do you honestly suppose it will be that easy? Your so-called friends are a bunch of snobs, Julia. Your own sister would have been dropped like a hot potato if I'd sent those gambling slips to her fiancé—oh yes, and that's why you came to the casino all dolled up and ready to impress the management with your high-class accent and your Van Holden name. What happened when you recognised me, my dear? Did your heart turn over?'

She gave him a scathing look. 'You were a horrid child and I knew the moment I saw you again that you'd grown into a hard, ruthless man. You keep saying you meant to give me those gambling slips, but I don't believe you. All you wanted was to drag a Van Holden down in the dirt——'

'Be quiet!' His hand shot out and grasped her around the nape of the neck. 'Whatever motivated the happenings of that night, I won't have them referred to as dirty.'

'Why not, Rome?' She could feel his fingers pressing into her nape. 'Is it your precious child you're thinking of? Are you trying to pretend to yourself that it was made with love?'

'At least with passion,' he said grimly. 'We weren't strangers, Julia. Do you think I didn't know that you used to watch me when I came to your grandmother's house to run her errands? You used to be playing on the lawn with your doll's pram and you'd let your long hair swing half over your face so you could watch me come along the back path to the kitchen door. I knew because I watched you as well. We were curious about each other even then, and that night in Naples was inevitable and you know it.'

'You made it happen,' she said indignantly. 'You knew I

was a—a good girl, but that didn't stop you, did it?'

'Did you really want me to stop?' The grip of his hand forced her to look at him. 'Come on, tell the truth and shame the devil.'

'There's no shame in you or the devil.' She could feel him urging her nearer all the time to his mouth and when his lips suddenly closed on hers she could taste the sweetness of the fig on them, and the lingering way he kissed her was sensuous as the way he had eaten the fruit.

'You have lovely lips,' he murmured. 'They weren't made for the bitter little things you say with them—come, try kissing me, you might enjoy the experience.'

'Go to the devil,' she muttered, trying to twist away from him and finding to her dismay that with hardly any effort he had made her take a reclining position so he was leaning over her, his eyes scanning her face and travelling down to the agitated movement of her breast under the silk of her robe.

'You smell of lilac scent and buttered corn,' he smiled, lowering his mouth to the soft hollow of her throat. 'Did Wineman ever kiss you like this, eh? Did he ever tell you that your skin has a crushable softness and that there's a kind of throb in your voice that makes you sound warm and sensual? Did he ever make you tremble when he touched you?'

'I—I'm trembling because you terrify me——'

'Don't talk nonsense.' His lips pushed aside the opening of her robe, making her gasp as he ran his lips over the smooth curve of her breast, his face resting warm against her. Suddenly his breath quickened; he rose to his feet and swept her up with him.

'I'm afraid I have to say to hell with your scruples, my dear.' He carried her from the *salone* into the bedroom and when he laid her down on the bed he held her there and gazed down intently into her eyes, the pupils of his own eyes darkly expanded into the smoky grey. 'Hate me if you have to, *carina*, but don't fight me. You're my wife and I'm going to have you whether you give or hold back. I'm going to take if you aren't woman enough to be generous.'

'You'll always have to take, Rome.' She lay there passively, for it was useless trying to fight him. 'I haven't a thing to give you.'

'You think not, my sweet?' He brushed a hand down her body. 'You have my baby under your heart and when I hold you I shall have the two of you in my arms.'

Julia turned her head away from him and flung an arm across her eyes. She heard him go into the *salone* and turn out the lamps, and when he returned she listened tensely to the sound of him undressing.

'Aren't you getting into bed? he asked. 'Shall I tuck you in?'

She shook her head and sat up, pushing at her hair in a defeated way. Her nightdress lay across the satin-topped stool at the foot of the bed and when she reached for it she heard Rome give a brief laugh. Julia ignored him and went into the bathroom to put on the nightdress and brush her teeth. He joined her there and she was intensely aware of his hard maleness as he used his own toothbrush and rinsed his mouth.

'Don't you wear pyjamas?' she asked tensely.

'No, I find them too restricting.' He watched her through the wall mirror. 'I like to stretch out in bed and feel free.'

'Like an animal,' she muttered.

'Yes, my dear. *La belle et la bête*.'

Julia clenched her teeth. 'The Beast gave Beauty time to get used to him.'

'Until she saw him through the eyes of love?' Rome

looked quizzical. 'I don't think I can wait that long, *donna mia.*'

'You've no pity in you!' she exclaimed.

'I'd be ashamed to be Italian if all you aroused in me was pity.' His hand swept her hair from her brow and his eyes ran over her in the delicate nightdress. '*Santo Dio,* don't look at me like that! I'm not a monster!'

'Please, Rome——' She backed away from his flagrant strength, his hard long limbs and wide shoulders. 'Give me time! I came to Italy as your wife believing you'd keep your word a-and just be kind——'

'I don't feel kind when I'm alone with you, *mia.*' His arms reached out and he gathered her completely against him, pressing her to his body. 'You see how it is, so be reasonable and don't act like a child. I can't treat you like one and that's a fact.'

'You promised——'

'Promises are abstract, my sweet, but you are warm and real—and I want you! Come, little one, let me love you!' And without further words he swept her up in his arms and carried her to bed.

He reached out from the bed and put out the lamp, plunging the room into a milky gloom. A cry of protest rose in Julia, a need to show fight, and fiercely she drove her fingernails into the supple skin of Rome's shoulders. He caught his breath audibly as her nails raked his back, jerking a little away from her to meet her eyes in the shafting moonlight.

'Does that make you feel better?' he demanded.

'I hope it hurt you!' She glared up at him, her eyes as trapped and green as a vixen's.

'You little fool, Julia, we could have fun——'

'Fun?' she exclaimed. 'Do you think I was amused when I found myself pregnant from your last bit of fun? You made me ill with your hot mouth and your hands all over me! If I'd known in New York that I'd have to endure more of it, I'd have done anything rather than marry you!'

'*Me ne frego*,' he said insolently. 'You did marry me and I don't give a damn for your ladylike sensibilities. I'm not Wineman and I don't intend to behave like him—if he'd been more of a man with you, then you might not be the little prig you are.'

'I do hate you!' Julia tossed her head back and forth on the pillow, tormented by her helplessness in his arms. 'I'd like to see you in hell! I pray for that, to make you go through the misery I went through when I found out what you'd done to me. I had a career and I had Paul—I loved Paul, do you hear? I still love him! He treated me in a way you know nothing about!'

'Like a precious painting, my dear? Or a rare porcelain to be handled with care?'

'He certainly didn't treat me like an object to be mauled!'

'*Grazie*.' Rome spoke through gritted teeth. 'All of a sudden, Julia, I have about as much desire for you as for a slice of cold pizza. Have the bed to yourself and your tepid dreams of Wineman. For what it's worth he won't want you now I've had you, no more than he'd want a classical vase with a handle missing.'

Rome swung himself out of bed and the moonlight glimmered on his tall body as he walked towards the door of his dressing-room. The door closed firmly behind him, but it was some moments before Julia stopped trembling from the reaction of their quarrel. Never in her life had she been party to such bitterness; it left her shaken and sick to her stomach, and with a little groan she drew up her legs and lay in a defensive, almost childish attitude.

She couldn't bear Rome to touch her when she hated him so much. He had ruined her chances with Paul ... she had wanted the kind of life Paul would have given her; cool, orderly and elegant.

She'd fight Rome all the way for trying to make her his kind of woman when she wanted to be Paul's!

CHAPTER FIVE

JULIA studied herself in the full-length Venetian mirror. She wore white cotton jeans and a bright, scoop-necked shirt that hung outside the jeans. She could no longer zip them up at the waist and had closed the gap as much as possible with a safety pin. Her hair was looped back at her nape in a green ribbon, and in the months she had been at Domani her skin had tanned softly in the Italian sunlight. In contrast to her honeyed skin her eyes were luminously green, and despite the fullness of her body she looked curiously young . . . more girlish than she had looked before her marriage.

Suddenly through the mirror she saw Lucie enter the bedroom and turned to smile at her. 'My clothes are becoming a problem,' she said. 'Rome filled the wardrobe with smart dresses, but just like a man he forgot that I wouldn't be able to get into them after a while. Do I look awfully fat?'

Lucie ran her eyes over Julia and shook an indulgent head. 'Being like that suits you—yes, it does, miss, so don't pull a face. It's true you don't look so elegant, but you look—wholesome, rather like that bread Cosenza bakes.'

'Thanks very much,' Julia laughed. 'It's nice to know that I'm going around looking like a loaf of bread!'

'It's golden-brown and tasty,' Lucie shook and folded Julia's nightdress, 'and I've seen the *signore* looking at you as if he'd like to take a nice big bite out of you.'

Julia slipped her feet into raffia sandals and bit her lip. She didn't know how much Lucie suspected about her lack of intimate relationship with Rome, and though for the sake of appearance she sometimes thumped a hollow into the pillow next to her own in an attempt to make it look as if he had shared her bed, it had to be obvious to her personal maid that they weren't sleeping together. Julia made the excuse that she was a restless sleeper now she was pregnant and he didn't like the way she fidgeted in the night and preferred his divan in the adjoining room.

Some weeks earlier Lucie had discovered that Julia was going to have his baby, and if she wondered why they were no longer on intimate terms she kept her thoughts discreetly to herself. She did remark that Julia's child looked all set to be spoiled by an indulgent father if the nursery was anything to go by.

The bright airy room Rome had chosen for the nursery had been painted and papered, carpeted in a thick curly floor covering, and a charming suite of infant furniture had been brought by delivery van all the way from Naples. Along with the furniture had come a stock of toys that would see the child from infancy to the schoolroom. When the train set was unpacked and its tracks laid along the gallery by Rome, Julia just had to remind him that there was no guarantee he was going to have a son.

Sprawled there on the floor admiring the trains, he had glanced up at her, smiling a little, a strand of black hair in his eyes. 'If we have a daughter,' he said, 'then I'll play with the trains myself.'

'You big fool!' Even yet Julia could feel an odd catch in her throat, aware that as a child Rome hadn't known what it was like to own a replica of the Rome Express and a full set of shunting cars. His mother had fed and clothed him and kept him in the best of health, but there had been no money left over for toys, and these that Rome brought with him from Naples were an assurance that his own child wouldn't go short of things to play with.

Now and again she came upon him strolling about in the nursery, looking intensely dark and tall as he handled the soft blankets on the cot and examined the tiny pastel garments in the chest of drawers painted with Beatrix Potter characters from her delightful little books, which were as popular in Italy as they were in America.

As the weeks had progressed Julia's resentment of the baby had lost its edge and she knew that she wanted no harm to befall it. But she still meant to leave Rome. There was no reality to a marriage such as theirs. They had merely struck a bargain and he had to abide by it ... he had to release her when the time came so she could try and pick up the threads of the life she really wanted.

Being here at Domani was just a necessary interlude, and these past weeks had shown her that it was the child whom Rome wanted, and loved. It was part of him, part of Italy, and she was merely the alien woman who carried the baby and would eventually give birth to it.

Initial shame and anger had made her believe that she could do something that would destroy the life that was growing in her, but such a thought no longer entered her head. Rome would have his child if all went well, and then their marriage of convenience would be over. He had surely learned that she had no intention of being a physical object in a man's life, and that was all a woman was if the man didn't love her. Marriage meant a companionship of the spirit as well as the body, and she and Rome were like enemies who had agreed to a truce, and that truce wouldn't survive beyond the next few months. Animosity would flare up again if he tried to hold her a prisoner at the villa, using the baby as a weapon at her head.

Julia was concerned that the baby be born whole and healthy, but she couldn't forgive the way Rome had forced her into his arms, making unrestrained love to her, using all his sensual power to make her respond to him, and she couldn't bury deep enough the memory of her body's response to his . . . a response she had tried so hard to fight as she lay in his arms and was consumed by the demands of the flesh.

Rome had made her have this baby without love, and there was a deep romanticism in Julia which made her cry when she listened to the lyrical music of *La Bohème* or the passionate splendour of *Tristan und Isolde*.

She could hardly bear at times the recollection that Rome had used her for his loveless pleasure . . . it must never happen again, and so far she had kept him at arm's length and this was probably due to the fact that she was now showing the presence of his baby. When he had desired her at Naples her figure had been slim and lissom, but a man had to be in love with a woman to feel that kind of desire for a body that was being pulled out of shape by a growing infant.

Lucie had just implied that Rome sometimes looked at her as if he'd like to eat her, but Lucie was a woman who devoured romantic novels in bed at night, along with her beloved custard creams, and Julia cynically told herself that what she really saw was an Italian looking with anticipation at the container of his son or daughter. Julia had seen for herself the flick of his eyes over the swell of her body. He couldn't wait, and she sensed it more and more, to hold in his arms what he had made with his big graceful body.

The child would be his assurance that he had a family again, but his interest in herself was no more than skin deep. Julia felt convinced there were other women with whom he satisfied his strong sensual needs, for often he stayed overnight in Naples. Once, rather to her chagrin, she had found herself seeking the tang of perfume on a shirt he had flung down before going to take a bath, but all she had detected on the linen was the aroma of cigar smoke and the healthy sweat from his body.

Rome was shrewd, of course, and Julia told herself that he'd hardly return home wearing a shirt upon which some other woman had left her fragrance. In his apartment above the casino he had clothes and all the comforts of home, and Julia couldn't quite control the images that went through her mind on those nights he spent away from the villa.

'I'm handy with a needle and thread,' said Lucie, breaking in on Julia's thoughts. 'I'll have a look through your wardrobe and see if there are any pleats and seams that I can let out for you. You don't want to go around looking unglamorous. The *signore* won't like that, being such a man of style. I've never seen a man who could wear his clothes so well, and he believes in buying the best, doesn't he?'

'Compensation for a deprived boyhood,' Julia replied. 'From the look of him now I would imagine his mother went without in order to make sure that he was nourished. He does have superb bones and teeth,' she added grudgingly.

'And I expect he's passed those on to the infant,' said Lucie, with a meaning look at Julia's waistline. 'You never say whether you want a boy or a girl, Miss Julia. Haven't you a preference? Some women have quite strong feelings about it. I always remember my sister couldn't stand the thought of having a boy. Her husband used to laugh and say it was that bit extra she'd have to wash if they had a boy.'

'Did it turn out to be a boy?' Julia smiled.

'No, she had a girl. They say if you wish hard enough

you get your wish. I bet the *signore* is hoping for a son. Italian men like that, the first time.'

Julia's pulses gave a throb. 'This is the first and last time!' she exclaimed, before she could put a rein on the words.

Lucie gave her a protesting look, and Julia shrugged her shoulders. 'I—I don't like being out of shape,' she said. 'Women don't have hordes of children these days, and I don't think I'm the maternal type.'

'You won't know how you'll be until you have the baby in your arms,' Lucie said reasonably. 'Babies bring love with them.'

'I—I don't want to talk about having it.' Julia pressed a hand to her stomach. 'The queasiness first thing in the morning is bad enough, but it's worn off now and I think I'll go and have some breakfast. I'll be very grateful, Lucie, if you do let out a few dresses for me. Perhaps I can help you?'

'When I remember those grubby, crooked seams you sewed as a child, miss, I think it will be best if I decline your offer. You go and have a nice big breakfast—the *signore* is off on business today, isn't he?'

Julia nodded. 'So he said last night. I expect there's more fun to be had in Naples.'

'I'm sure he'd take you with him if you wanted to go, Miss Julia.'

'You think the sun shines out of him, don't you?' Julia's eyes were suddenly storm-green. 'He certainly has what it takes to make some of you women weak in the head!'

'You're anatomy's all wrong, miss, it's in the knees. And, begging your pardon, you must have lost control of your knees one fine night!'

'Lucie!' Julia wanted to be angry, but she relied too much on Lucie's kindness and goodwill to reprimand her for what she took to be the truth. Julia couldn't have borne for anyone to know the real truth, that it hadn't been love which had brought her into collision with Rome ... that there had been no moon shining in a velvet sky and no whispered words of longing. He had collected payment for a gambling debt, and he had made sure of the interest rate!

'Were you terribly shocked, Lucie, when you realised I was having this baby and that its conception had taken place before my marriage to Rome?'

'It's no crime for a couple to want each other, and I'm not narrow-minded, miss. Mr Rome married you, and that's the main thing.'

'Do you really think so?' Julia couldn't help looking cynical. She had wanted Paul Wineman and the orderly, elegant life they would have shared, with none of the heated emotion which underlay her connection with Rome. She didn't love him, but because they were husband and wife she couldn't help but be suspicious of the life he led when he was absent from Domani. She resented his child inside her, yet she obeyed all the instructions given her by the obstetrician who came to see her once a month. She drank pints of milk and orange juice, took her vitamins regularly and combined relaxation with sensible exercise. She wanted the child to be healthy, but she was terrified of loving it.

Julia fought those kind of feelings and was determined to leave Italy as soon as she was able to do so. She wouldn't allow herself to feel guilty about leaving Rome and the baby, no more than he had felt guilty that morning in Naples, watching her leave his apartment with a slight smile at the edge of his mouth, as if he already knew that the humbling of Blanche Van Holden's granddaughter had only just begun.

'I'm going down to have my breakfast.' Julia made her

way to the door, for if she stayed here another moment she would blurt out to Lucie that she hated Rome and was going to abandon the baby to him as soon as it was born. Lucie would do her utmost to dissuade her; she would underline words like motherhood and duty, and Julia fled from them in her own mind, hastening down the stairs to the hall.

When she walked out on to the sunlit *terrazza* she felt an instant clutch of dismay, for Rome was seated at the table, a newspaper spread open in his hands. When she neared the table she heard him utter an imprecation.

'That's a nice greeting, I must say!'

He glanced up from the paper and met her eyes. '*Santo Dio*, but it's annoying! Our team sat on a single goal against Holland when they should have attacked them for a few more.'

'World-shattering,' she murmured as she sat down.

'*Si.*' He inclined his head. 'Now Italy haven't a chance for the Cup.'

'What a catastrophe!' Julia poured coffee and added plenty of cream, then took a look under the lid of the silver warmer to see if Rome had left her any bacon. She always had a fancy for it when that morning queasiness wore off, and to her delight there were several slices of crisp fried bacon, a couple of sausages and little button mushrooms. 'Delicious!'

'Have some fruit first.' Rome was looking at her as he flicked a hand at a basket of golden medlars, plump nectarines and a couple of melons.

'A slice of melon,' she decided, and was reaching for it when he touched her wrist and fingered the gold gate-bracelet she always wore, with the little heart attached.

'Allow me.' He took the melon and cut it in half, scooped out the seeds from the socket and added a large spoonful of honey. As he placed the melon in front of her, his eyes flicked her sun-touched hair. 'You're looking very well, Julia. The baby doesn't trouble you in any way?'

'I always feel as if I could be sick when I first wake up.' She took a mouthful of the sweet juicy fruit and as she ate it was conscious of his gaze upon her lips. 'Lucie removes my pillows and makes me lie flat and still and the heaves gradually fade away.'

'It can't be very pleasant for you,' he said, with a touch of concern.

'None of this has been a picnic for me, Rome.' She took a bread roll, fresh and fragrant from the oven, and broke it in half. He handed her the butter dish and she noticed how brown his hand was in contrast to the creamy butter. She took a bite of the bread and remembered what Lucie had said, that she had a wholesome look and that Rome sometimes looked as if he'd like to bite her. Julia met his eyes and told herself it was the sun on her skin that made her feel suddenly hot.

'If men,' she said, 'had to feel sick each morning and go around looking like a lump, there would be a sudden drop in the population count.'

His lips quirked at the edge and his eyes held glints of sunlight that added to their brilliance in his lean Italian face. 'I would hardly say that you look lumpy, *mia*. You—you remind me of the way you looked when you were a small girl, your hair in a ribbon, a smear of jam on your mouth, pushing a cat about in a pram.'

'Really, Rome, don't get sentimental.' Julia didn't want him to refer to the days of their childhood, when they had both been innocent and she hadn't known why her grandmother said she wasn't to play with the cleaning woman's boy. She had liked his eyes and had wanted to sit with him on the smooth green grass and see him smile and dip his hand in her bag of jelly beans.

'Don't get hard, Julia,' he rejoined. 'You couldn't look as you do and be totally unhappy here at Domani.'

'It's a nice house.' She shook a little tomato sauce on to her bacon and sausages. 'I like swimming in the pool and lazing about in the sun and strolling in the garden. I do my very best to forget why I'm really here, though it becomes more difficult as your child fills me out a bit more each day.'

'It's our child, part of both of us.' He spoke decisively as he spun the wheel of his lighter and lit a cheroot, puffing the smoke away from the table so it eddied over the *terrazza* wall.

'You sound as if you've been reading some of Lucie's romantic novels,' Julia said, giving him a cool-eyed look. 'You forced me into this condition, Rome, but you can't take control of my emotions. I give your child a warm nest to lie in and, I hope, health and strength from your excellent cuisine, but I have no more affection for it than I have for you. Nature hasn't worked some alchemy and made me love my seducer.'

'Julia, for the love of heaven!' His eyes flashed with sudden temper through the smoke of his cheroot. 'I won't have that word at my table!'

'I know another, Rome, much more basic.' She carried sausage to her mouth and chewed it appreciately. 'I'm getting so fat that Lucie is going to let out seams for me.'

'There's no need for that,' he said. 'I can have some smart maternity outfits sent from Naples.'

'Why can't I come with you and choose them?' she found herself asking.

'Do you want to come?' His eyes had narrowed as he looked at her and she could actually see the tension of his shoulders, as if he were preparing to reject any real desire on her part to go with him.

'No,' she said indifferently. 'I prefer being here at Domani on my own, and there are such a lot of dresses in my wardrobe that Lucie, I assure you, will do more than let out a few seams. I hate maternity smocks and things, they don't really hide anything but make you look bulgier in other places. No, I'll stay here. I haven't any interest in what goes on at the casino, and as they say, two's company and three is none.'

'I beg your pardon!' His cheroot was arrested midway to his lips.

'You have good ears, *signore*, you heard what I said.'

'The full meaning of your remark escapes me, so please explain yourself.'

'You know very well what I mean, so don't quiz me.'

'I can guess what you're implying and I want an explanation.' He snapped his fingers. *'Pronto!'*

'Really, Rome, I'm not a naïve fool—not any more.' She gave him a scornful smile. 'I haven't had the displeasure of your company at bedtime since we came here to the villa, so there has to be someone who provides you with your—fun.'

The instant she spoke Julia felt a stab of fear; he was so big and dark sitting there and the chalk-striped grey suit he wore added to his look of male power. Very deliberately he took a pull on his cheroot and drew down the smoke before releasing it from his taut nostrils, in that nerve-burning moment he studied her as if she were a gnat he was planning to squash. The sun gleamed on his thick dark hair, played over his features but couldn't find its way into the deep chin cleft. His face had a seriousness which made her accusation seem cheap and tawdry, and suddenly she couldn't bear his scrutiny a second longer and jumping to her feet she went to the wall of the *terrazza* and gazed down at the water, beaten silver in the sunlight, the beach meandering beside it into the distance.

'So you think I have a girl-friend in Naples,' he said quietly. 'Does the idea make you jealous?'

'Not at all,' she said. 'There could only be jealousy if I cared for you, and you happen to know my feelings. I don't care a fig what you do when you're in Naples so long as I don't have to be pestered by you. You can have a dozen girl-friends for all I care.'

'What if I had one here in Campania?' he drawled. 'What would you say to that, my dear?'

Julia locked her hands upon the wall, feeling the iron spears under her fingers, hot with the sun and cemented into the stone as a safeguard against anyone sitting on the parapet with its long, fateful drop to the beach and the rocks.

'Nothing you did would surprise me, Rome,' she replied, watching the glint of the sun on her bracelet. It made her think of the mother she could barely remember; the bracelet had belonged to her along with the gold heart neck chain which had been given to Verna. What, she wondered, would have been the course of their lives had their parents not been killed? Her mother had been English so they might have gone there to live and then she would never have met Rome Demario.

'But it would affront your dignity, Julia.' His chair moved on the flagstones as he stood up and strolled to where she stood, tall above her figure and the pale shine of her hair. He stood behind her and she felt him to the base of her backbone though he made no attempt to touch her.

'I—I hardly feel dignified any more, not with this constant reminder of you that I have to carry around. I wish it could all be over! I wish the days away, do you know that?'

'It's natural,' he murmured. 'I realise that the baby grows heavier and you are only a slender girl. His fingers touched her looped hair and moved underneath to the softness of her nape. The shock of his fingers on her was more than she could bear and she swung round in order to dislodge his hand, which slid to her shoulder and then to the contour of her breast.

'Don't!' she gasped, her eyes reflecting the shock that went through her body as he fondled her. 'How dare you?'

'I am your husband.' He smiled as he said it and that set a fierce little flame to her temper. She lashed out with her hand and caught him across the throat, making him catch his breath rather sharply. She drew away from him, the pupils of her eyes hugely dilated as she watched him massage the place she had struck. She had meant to slap his face but the blow had gone astray, finding one of the vulnerable parts of his strong body. Irrationally she wanted to say she was sorry, but the words wouldn't come ... it really served him right for touching her . . . like that.

'A touch of Karate, eh?' His lip twisted into a brief smile. 'I wonder why you didn't try that in Naples?'

'It was just an unlucky blow——' She bit her lip. 'I wish to goodness I had thought of it in Naples!'

Rome merely looked at her, his eyes upon the swell of her body.

'Do you know what I wish whenever you leave this house?' She felt as if his eyes were seeing the actual strain upon her where his child was resting.

'That I shall drive off the highway and with any luck break my neck?'

'No! It's just that I wish you'd live at the casino a-and leave me in peace.'

'I see.' He quizzed what was left of his cheroot and deliberately crushed it out between his hard fingertips. 'Does my presence here so disturb you, Julia? Is that why you sometimes roam from your bedroom at night and sit on your balcony?'

'I—get restless when the baby moves inside me.'

'You never think to call me in—I might be able to help you sleep.'

'I call Lucie, thank you!' A flush stung her cheeks, for there seemed in his words a hint that he would make love to her and make her drowsy that way.

'And what does she do?' He raised a sardonic eyebrow. 'Talk with you about the days when you were a pampered little girl and I was the slum kid with his nose pressed up against the windows of your house on Grand Drive?'

'We talk,' Julia admitted, 'but not about you. I've tried not to shatter the romantic image Lucie has of you, Rome. It rather amuses me to listen to the superlatives about my husband and all the trouble he goes to making sure I have the best of everything in my delicate condition. I do believe that Lucie thinks I'm the luckiest girl alive to have such a handsome and thoughtful husband, but I know what you're really like, don't I, *signore*?'

'What am I really like, my dear?' He lounged against the parapet wall and with the sunlit sky behind him, his eyes became shaded by his black lashes and brows.

'A devil who trades on his charm,' she replied, and thought again how alike he was to that painting of the underworld lord who carried off Proserpina as she plucked flowers in a field.

'So you think I have charm—that at least is encouraging.'

'It's a natural perquisite of Italian men,' she rejoined. 'Look at your gardener!'

'I fear it doesn't come natural to me, looking at other men. Do you often look at him, my dear?'

'Why not?' She gave a flippant laugh. 'He's so obviously on show with his bare torso and his neck chain, not to mention his tattoo.'

'Julia,' Rome spoke her name softly, 'don't ever encourage the attentions of other men.'

'When I'm like this?' She swept an expressive hand down her figure. 'Don't you Italian people call this a state of grace, which makes me holy and untouchable except by——' She bit her lip. 'There's only one man whose attentions I sought and you—you made it seem as if I was one sort of person at the gallery, and another sort behind his back. You never gave me a chance to speak privately with Paul——'

'What would you have told him?' A rather brutal note came into Rome's voice. 'That you were seven weeks gone with the child of your dago lover?'

'Rome!'

'His sort likes his belongings all pristine and cool behind glass. He has the collector's obsession with chastity.'

'Haven't you?' she demanded. 'You've just implied that it would upset your sense of possession if I looked at another man.'

'You're my wife, but had I been in Wineman's shoes the day I told him you were marrying me, I'd have done a darned sight more than smoke a cigarette in a holder and offer polite congratulations. Especially if he had reason to believe you cared for him—and you say you did.'

'We were going out together and Paul knew I didn't socialise with a man unless I liked him.'

'Liked, my dear?'

'Loved,' she quickly corrected. 'I didn't expect Paul to be demonstrative—he's rather a shy man and extremely courteous. We had a lot in common and our companionship was congenial. You wouldn't understand——'

'No,' Rome agreed. 'The idea of being with an attractive woman and treating her as if she might break if I breathed on her is certainly a mystery to me. In my experience women like to be shown they have sex appeal.'

'As I've mentioned before, Rome,' Julia's voice had sharpened, 'don't confuse me with your other women. I'm sure they're legion, but you will recall that I didn't throw myself into your arms. I did my utmost to get out of them!'

'I wonder, Julia, why you insist on believing yourself a frigid woman? Maybe you felt you had to react like that with Wineman, but now you're with me, and I'm a very different sort of man.'

No two men could have been more dissimilar, she thought, not only in appearance but in their attitudes to life. There was in Rome a vital need for what was alive and sensuous; he was impatient of the things that gave pleasure to Paul; works of art didn't breathe and couldn't feel and so he dismissed the painted flower for the real one; the sheen on porcelain for the warmth of a woman's skin.

'You're an earth subject, Rome,' she said. 'It has nothing to do with your upbringing, for I don't imagine you'd have been sensitive to art had you been reared in the National Gallery.'

'I don't know whether to accept that as a compliment or an insult. Anyway,' he glanced at the gold quartz watch on a leather strap dark as the hairs of his wrist, 'intriguing as the subject is, I have to be on my way to Naples.'

And then, before she realised his intention, he drew her into his arms and holding her with firm insistence found her mouth with his. His kiss was purposeful, parting her lips and making her accept the sensual intimacy for endless moments.

Then he put her away from him and gave her a brief

bow. '*Arrivederci, carina.* I shall be gone about three days, so take care!'

Julia watched silently as he strode from the *terrazza*, tall and dark in his stylish grey suit, leaving her with a hand pressed to her body as his child moved so disturbingly deep within her. Three days, he had said, and he had neither admitted nor denied that he had a girl waiting for him in Naples.

The stillness was such that she heard the roar of his car when he drove away from Domani. He would drive at full speed along the highway, taking those sweeping curves with nerveless skill. He was admittedly the most alive person Julia had ever known, and as she edged her tongue around the sensitivity of her soundly kissed lips she wondered what a woman felt when she abandoned herself without reservation to the passion in Rome.

As the silence settled around her Julia turned to gaze at the sea, so deep and boundless under that calm-looking surface, but so dangerous if it wasn't treated with caution. Rome was like that, she realised. He was deep and vital with forces it was dangerous to disturb, and yet when she was with him she felt driven to disturb him until the atmosphere between them was tense as a live wire that might snap furiously at any moment.

With Paul she had never felt like that; she had listened attentively when he talked of art and literature in his cultured voice, aware that he thought her as elegant and cool as the jade he collected. She had known how much he liked her when he told her that she reminded him of his favourite piece of jade, the oriental goddess which he had purchased while on a trip to Peking, which had pride of place in a softly lit niche of a carved cabinet three centuries old.

Paul wouldn't think now that she reminded him of his jade goddess, and Julia smiled ruefully as she moved a hand against her body. He wasn't the type of man to care much for children, he had too many rare and lovely objects in his apartment and was too sophisticated to lounge on the floor and romp with a child, building a house of bricks, fitting together the trucks of a train set, or reading about gnomes from a book which was sticky from jammy fingers.

Julia stood lost in thought there in the warm sunlight, mesmerised a little by the silvery flicker of the sea. She felt a sense of unreality, as if there had been a subtle change in her personality so that she found it hard to associate herself with the poised saleslady she had been, clad in a slim-fitting dark blue dress, handling objects as if they were more precious than people.

A sigh escaped her . . . she felt so mixed up, and the only certainty was that Rome was to blame; he was the culprit who did this to her and was unaffected himself by the changes taking place in her. He came and went and ran his life along chosen lines he didn't allow anyone to disrupt, and it was his freedom that Julia envied. He had tied her down, but his own wings were as unclipped as they had ever been and even as she stood here, he was speeding to a rendezvous which she felt convinced had nothing to do with the casino.

'Signora?'

Julia came out of her reverie with a start and turned from the parapet to find Giovanni's daughter looking at her in some curiosity. Maddalena was sloe-eyed and her skin was smooth as honey; her earlobes were pierced by small gold rings and she was audaciously pretty and very aware of her effect on men. It hadn't escaped Julia's notice that the girl flirted with Rome, who accepted the attention in a lazily amused way. Julia naturally wondered if his attention was less indolent when she wasn't present at one of his encounters with Maddalena. As the girl's parents had worked at the villa for three years, he had known her since she was a schoolgirl and he would hardly have failed to notice that she had grown up to be extremely attractive.

As Julia gazed enquiringly at Maddalena she recalled Rome's answer when she had asked if he had a girl-friend in Naples. 'What if I had one in Campania?'

Maddalena glanced at the *terrazza* table where Rome's newspaper lay crumpled. 'The *signore* has left already for Naples?' she asked. 'He promised to take with him my crucifix and chain to be repaired.'

'He was in rather a hurry,' Julia said drily. 'I expect he'll take your trinket with him the next time he goes there. Can't someone in the village mend it for you? There's that little shop where clocks and watches are repaired——'

Maddalena shook her head so the sun caught her earrings. 'It was purchased in Naples by the *signore* when I had my eighteenth birthday. It is gold—Tullio broke the clasp with his clumsiness and when I told the *signore* he said at once that he would see to it that it was repaired as good as new. I very much value it, you see.' The girl blinked her long dark lashes and ran her hands down the taut sides of her fawn-coloured dress, with lace edging the short sleeves. She refused to wear the cap that matched the dress, and Julia applied no pressure on the girl. She had glossy hair with a natural wave in it, and Julia had long ago developed a dislike of servility, stemming from that day when Grandma Van Holden had so curtly dismissed Rome's mother from her employ.

'You spoke of Tullio's clumsiness,' Julia said. 'I hope he doesn't bully you in any way. He looks a very tough young man.'

'He forgets his own strength,' Maddalena replied, a smile curling on her lips. 'And he is also jealous because the *signore* gave me a present of gold.'

'That was generous of the *signore.*' Suddenly the slim shapeliness of the girl made Julia very conscious of the own loss of grace, and she felt a stab of resentment that of all the women in his life Rome had to ensure that she bore the brunt of his passionate lovemaking. Others got away with trinkets, but she got saddled with his progeny, and from the feel of the infant it was going to take after him for size!

'There is no one as nice as the *signore.*' Maddalena let her eyes rest on Julia's waistline. 'You must be very proud, *signora,* to be having his son.'

'It could well be a daughter,' Julia replied, though somehow she had the instinctive feeling that she carried a boy.

Maddalena smiled and shook her head. 'A man like that, he has a son the first time, *signora.* We notice it a lot in Italy. The men are very definite, you see, very masculine, and they like to establish the family name. The *signore* will make a very good father.'

'What makes you so sure of that?' Julia asked curiously.

'Because he is kind.' Maddalena looked surprised by the question. 'The *signora* must know better than anyone how kind he can be. When his mother was here at the villa he was as good with her as the nurses she had to have when her illness grew worse. He would sit with her at night and hold her in his arms, and that was how she died, peacefully and quietly with him, and later when I took coffee to him in his study he was sitting there at his desk, having arranged the funeral, and there were tears on his face. He didn't try to hide them. Real men cry when they are hurt, and we all knew how much he loved his mother. Every day until the burial there were flowers in her room, masses of them, especially lilacs which she very much liked. In his black suit at the funeral he looked so tall and sad and distinguished—it's a shame he didn't have a wife at the time to console him. He lived away from the villa for quite a long time and we feared he might sell it. My parents like working for him and the village people like to think of him as their *padrone*.'

'I thought that was a position of heritage,' Julia said.

'Not always, *signora*. Country people will apply the title to a man they respect and admire.'

'He runs a gambling casino!' Julia exclaimed.

'*Sí*, but who in Italy doesn't gamble?' Maddalena made an expressive gesture with her hands. 'If you were not the wife of the *signore*, then most of the village would be holding bets as to whether you carry a boy or a girl.'

'It must have come as a disappointment to everyone when he brought home an American wife?' Julia couldn't help wondering how much of a disappointment it had been for the pretty Maddalena. She made no secret of her admiration for Rome and seemed to regard him as someone to be looked up to. Julia didn't doubt the care and kindness he had lavished upon his mother, but that didn't excuse him in her eyes. He was still the man who had been merciless towards her on account of an incident in their childhood; all his growing years he had harboured his grudge until he found an opportunity to satisfy it. She had no reason to respect and admire him!

'A lot of the girls were disappointed,' Maddalena said unsmilingly. Her gaze dwelt consideringly upon Julia and she obviously knew that Julia had become pregnant some time before her wedding day. 'Of course, the *signore* would marry a woman if he had to do so.'

With these rather insolent words she went to the breakfast table and began to pile the crockery on to a tray. Julia should have reprimanded her, but it seemed absurd to take someone to task for speaking the truth. Rome had married her because he had to . . . they had never exchanged words of love, and if there was a girl in Campania who loved him, then she had been badly let down.

'Tullio wished to know if you would like roses for the *salone*?' Maddalena stood there holding the laden tray, so darkly pretty in her fawn dress that she might well have fancied her chance of becoming the mistress of the villa.

'Yes, roses always look best when they're cut and used in the house. You can arrange them, Maddalena. I'm going down to the beach for a couple of hours.'

'But you can't, *signora*! The *signore* said he didn't like the look of those steps and you weren't to use them until the cliffside was shored up——'

'I shall be careful. It's such a lovely morning and I want to laze in the sun and breathe the sea air.'

'But, *signora*, if anything happened to you while the *signore* is absent he would blame us for not taking proper care of you—and the child.'

It was Maddalena's mention of the precious child that decided Julia. The beach looked too inviting to resist, and the cliffs weren't likely to shift until the next rainfall. It had been the heavy rain of the other evening which had caused a slippage of earth and rock, but for the past two days the weather had been flawless.

'I shall take care and see that no harm comes to the son and heir,' she said lightly.

'Why not rest by the pool, *signora*, or take a swim in it?'

Julia took a look below at the beach whose sands looked like warm tawny velvet upon which she had an urge to stretch out. 'I want to feel the sand between my toes.'

'Tullio can always fetch up a bucketful for you to tread in,' said Maddalena, with a touch of humour.

Julia smiled, but felt obstinately disinclined to be told she must stay up here in the villa when she felt like enjoying the beach. Who, she thought cynically, would have cared what risks Rome's foreign wife took if she hadn't been carrying his child?

'I'm going indoors to fetch a few things. Don't try and thwart a mother-to-be, next time I might demand pickles and jam.'

'*Signora*——'

'Take the dishes to the kitchen, Maddalena, then go and talk to Tullio while he cuts the roses. You're a lucky girl, you know. He's very good-looking.'

'And he knows it,' Maddalena retorted.

'Don't they all!' Julia walked from the *terrazza* into the hall, and as she passed one of the onyx tables she saw a letter lying on a salver and paused to examine the envelope in case it was addressed to her. It was pale mauve, expensively thick, and Rome's name was upon it and the handwriting was a woman's. Julia put it to her nose and smelled a delicate perfume. She set her lips and examined the postmark—Madrid. Spain! Her devoted husband certainly believed in spreading wide his net! She returned the letter to the salver and continued on her way to the bedroom, where she was collecting together such items as a sunhat and sun-oil when Lucie came into the room carrying a sewing-box.

'That's right, miss,' she said, 'you relax in the sun by the pool. It will do you the world of good, especially as you didn't get much sleep last night.'

'I'm going down to the beach,' Julia said casually.

There was a significant silence, and then Lucie placed the sewing-box on the bed stool and returned to the door, where she stood firmly against the handle. 'Over my dead body, miss,' she said.

'Please get away from the door.' Julia could feel herself beginning to tremble slightly. The beach had become an issue, and all because of the baby ... it wouldn't do for anything to happen to Rome's baby!

'Please move out of my way,' Julia said tensely.

'No, miss!' Lucie had set her stocky body determinedly against the door. 'That cliffside has become hazardous and you know it! You could be hurt—why, I'd never forgive myself if any harm came to you!'

'You mean the baby, don't you?' Julia had gone so pale that only her eyes seemed to hold any colour. 'Rome's precious infant!'

'Don't talk like that, Miss Julia. The baby means just as much to you and you wouldn't want to hurt it by risking yourself on those beach steps.'

'You think not?' Julia tossed her hair and hardened her eyes. 'I never wanted this child in the first place—he forced it upon me and I hate him, do you hear? I hate him!'

'Miss Julia!'

'If you knew what he did——'

'I don't believe Mr Rome ever did you a day's harm.'

'No, he did it at night, and he made sure I had nine months of misery to endure.' Suddenly the tears were spilling over and Julia no longer cared about pride and keeping her feelings to herself. 'Y-you can't imagine how unhappy I am! I'm a prisoner in this house, condemned to live here until I have the child before I can be free—and I mean to be free!'

Through her tears Julia saw the shocked, unbelieving look on Lucie's face, then generously she was holding open her arms and like a child again Julia was running into them, not with skinned knees or a broken toy, but with an aching and bewildered heart that needed comfort.

'My poor lovey,' Lucie stroked her hair, 'I could see there was something amiss between the two of you, but I never dreamed it was making you this miserable. So you married Mr Rome because you had to?'

Julia nodded and it was such a relief to have someone

at last to confide in. 'He ruined everything for me, Lucie. There was someone I liked so much, the sort of man who would have had Grandma's approval, and then this happened and I had no option but to marry Rome——'

'What I don't understand,' Lucie drew her brows together, 'you were never the sort of girl to get yourself into that kind of trouble. Miss Verna was more flighty in that way, but you—you were always such a proud little person, with respect for yourself and others that always made me extra fond of you. You weren't cut out for affairs with men——'

'There was no affair—not in the sense that Rome and I were seeing one another a-and were in love. I—I don't want to go into the details, except to say that I'm only staying with him until the baby's born. He wants the baby—I'm just incidental.'

'But you can't mean——?' Lucie scanned Julia's face. 'You can't give up your baby—it isn't in you!'

'Isn't it?' Julia smiled wryly and touched her stomach. 'He'd never let me take the baby with me and I mean to get away from him. He'll be a better provider than I. He has money and this house, and he likes the idea of being a father. That's the only redeeming thing about him, he wants his child and was horrified when I mentioned—anyway, he wouldn't let me go to a clinic for that sort of thing and insisted that I marry him. We struck a sort of bargain, you see.'

'Yes, miss.' Lucie looked at Julia as if she glimpsed the real cause of so much distress. 'Now why don't you wash your face and go and sit by the pool? For the time being, Miss Julia, the baby is your main concern and you know it, don't you? You can't hurt the innocent.'

'I—I was innocent.' Julia felt the blood rise in a wave of heat through her body. 'I'm justified in blaming Rome for all this. I can't be fooled by his charm like other people—I know how ruthless he can be. Life could have been so different for me, so orderly and nice, and now it's just a mess. Sometimes at night it all sweeps over me and I just don't know what to do—having a baby is different, Lucie, if there's love involved and there's someone you can turn to in the dark when the little fears start jabbing at you. I—I've never had a baby before and sometimes I'm afraid——'

'Hush now,' Lucie soothed. 'Take each day as it comes and don't keep asking questions of fate. I kept doing that when my Bert died, but you never get any satisfactory answers and only wear yourself out. Now you freshen up and go and relax in the sunshine until it's time for lunch. If you fancy anything special, Cosenza will be only too pleased to cook it for you. How about a nice lamb chop, little peas and some baked potatoes, with apple pie to follow? That was always your favourite meal in the old days.'

'The old days,' Julia sighed. 'We never realise how lucky we are when we're children and there's someone grown up to rely on. Had Grandma lived, none of this would have happened!'

'Who knows?' Lucie glanced around the big bedroom, with its cool, silvery beauty. 'Fate has us on a string, miss. We all get dangled in the lion's mouth one way or another, and the villa's a nice place when you look around it.'

'It's a gilded cage,' Julia said quietly. 'All of you are really on Rome's side, making a prisoner of me. You'll be on his side when the baby's born, won't you?'

'I don't take sides, miss. I just believe in common sense.'

'I believe you're talking about compromise,' Julia argued.

'Yes, miss.' Lucie held Julia's pained eyes with her own. 'A baby needs a mother and a father, and you should know that only too well.'

'I—I don't want to think about it! I don't want to talk

about it any more!' And turning away, Julia hastened into the bathroom to wash away her tears.

Compromise, she thought, gazing into the mirror and seeing the forlorn look that lurked about her mouth and in her eyes. Give in to Rome ... remain his wife for the sake of the child and know that whenever he felt the urge to see another woman he would do so. He didn't even care if they wrote to the villa on their scented notepaper.

She caught her breath as his child moved inside her, a flutter that was part of her and yet distinct from her, a presence that lived and grew in her, the tiny heart pumping away beneath her heart.

'Damn you, Rome!' she whispered tormentedly. 'Why couldn't you stay out of my life!'

There was no answer except another of those flutters in her body, that movement of the tiny limbs stretching and touching her, reminding her too vividly of the man in whose arms she had lain while on the waterfront at Naples someone sang a Neapolitan love song. Even yet she remembered the sound echoing on the water, while she learned from the warm lips on hers that desire has no mercy.

CHAPTER SIX

It seemed that everyone in the village was taking an interest in Julia's condition, and she was doing her best to get used to it. It seemed to be part of the local character and people had started to bring presents of little carved toys and knitted garments to the villa, along with home-made candy that was really delicious—candied cherries and figs, plums with a nut filling, sultana fudge and creamy toffee.

'I shall look like a plum duff before long!' Julia laughed, sharing the sweets with Lucie as in days gone by. 'The Campanians are such nice people, you can't help growing fond of them.'

'They're genuine,' Lucie said. 'They aren't spoiled by the artificial things too many city folk regard as essential, as if without machines and a psychoanalyst they couldn't survive.'

'You're my analyst, Lucie. What would I do without you?'

'Remember, miss, it was Mr Rome who thought you'd like the idea of having me here.'

'He knew he'd often be away on his little trips.'

'He has his business to think of.'

'A gambling casino can hardly be placed in that category. Everything he has,' Julia made a sweeping gesture with her hand, 'has been bought with the money a lot of foolish people lose at his gaming tables. Believe me, he has no conscience about it. He made up his mind a long time ago that he wasn't going to work like a slave and end up like his father.'

When Lucie looked enquiring Julia realised that Rome's mother had never talked of the circumstances of her widowhood.

'Rome's father died of overwork,' she said quietly, for it suddenly seemed wrong to abuse his confidence. 'Mr Demario tried to establish a small business and then fell ill and didn't recover.'

'Then it's understandable if Mr Rome chooses to make his living the way he does. No one forces people to gamble with their money and I'm sure the casino is honestly run and everything—I couldn't imagine the *signore* cheating anyone just to make himself rich.'

'Some people are weak, Lucie.' Julia sighed as she thought of her sister's lack of resistance to the fever of gambling. 'A casino to them is like this nut fudge to you and me, except that we know when we've had enough. I hate the casino! I wish I'd never seen the place!'

'You were bitten by the gambling bug?' Lucie looked surprised. 'That doesn't sound like you, Miss Julia, not that I'm saying you didn't like a bit of fun—do you remember when I used to take you and Miss Verna to Coney Island? Your eyes used to shine and I couldn't keep you off the helter-skelter——'

Lucie broke off and looked thoughtful a moment. 'It was Miss Verna who did the gambling, wasn't it?'

Julia nodded. 'I—I had to try and help her. She was engaged to Lawrence Hale, but I knew he wouldn't risk marrying a girl who lost hundreds of dollars playing roulette—you know the Hale family, they've always been in banking and the law. They wouldn't have stood for it, and it would have broken Verna's heart to lose Lawrence. I went to the casino to speak to the proprietor—I had no idea it was Rome. He suggested a way I could pay off the debt, but as you can see, Lucie, there was a little miscalculation, which everyone seems certain will be a boy. Most of those little knitted things are in blue——'

Julia broke off, for Giovanni was making his way towards the pool, carrying a mid-morning pot of tea on a tray. As he set it down on the little table beside Julia's lounger he told her that the shoring up work on the cliffs was completed and the beach steps had been cleared of rubble.

'Oh, good!' Julia smiled up at him. 'I've missed the feel of the sand and the sound of the sea moving in and out of the big groin of rock. Ask Cosenza to pack me a lunch basket, I'm going to spend the afternoon down there!'

'*Sí, signora.*' Giovanni returned her smile in his rather grave way.

'The steps are quite safe now?' Lucie demanded.

Giovanni inclined his head. 'Tullio has been down to take a look and he assures me everything is in order. We wouldn't allow the *signora* to take any unnecessary risks, especially with the *signore* away from home.'

Rome had been gone for a week, but he had not been in touch to say when he'd be home. 'I expect he got tied up with someone.' Julia poured tea and looked indifferent. 'I'm grateful to you, Giovanni, for getting the beach steps in order.'

'The *signore* left his orders. Is there anything special the *signora* would like for lunch?'

'Just lots of nice tasty things, and one of those crunchy pickles I like. Cosenza will know.'

Giovanni allowed his lips to quirk. 'Cosenza will not forget the pickle, *signora.*'

After he had gone Julia handed Lucie her cup of tea. 'Oh, don't look po-faced, I've missed going down to the beach. It does me good down there. I get plenty of fresh air.'

'You be careful, miss. There'd be hell to pay——'

'Would there?' Julia stirred her tea and looked cynical. 'What do you imagine he's doing right now? Sitting in his office doing the accounts?'

'Very likely.'

'I just can't seem to shake your hero-worship, can I?'

'If he's done wrong, miss, he's doing his best to make up for it. I've seen that for myself—a lot of young women would envy you for having him, and living in a place like this.'

'I happen to think there are more important things.' Julia sipped her tea and her gaze rested broodingly on the shimmering surface of the pool. 'You loved your husband, didn't you?'

'My Bert?' Lucie smiled, and then sighed. 'He was a good, kind man and no doubt that's how he came to die, helping others and not giving any thought to his own safety. Yes, there's something special about loving the man you live with, I'll grant you that, Miss Julia.'

'There's none of that between Rome and me—you must have realised that weeks ago.'

'I know he sleeps in his dressing-room.' Lucie looked directly at Julia. 'Some men are proud, and if you've shown him that you don't want him——'

'He knows well enough that I don't want him,' Julia said tersely. 'We aren't married in the true sense of the word, so don't speak to me as if I'm under some obligation to be a proper wife to him. I'll never give in to him—I'll fight him to the last ditch!'

'You could regret that, you know.'

'The thing I regret is that everything is over between me and Paul, the other man I told you about.'

'Are you sure?'

'Yes. Paul wanted me as I was. He could never accept the

fact that I've belonged to Rome and carried his child. He's too fastidious.'

'One of those, eh?' Lucie looked down her nose. 'The sort who likes to believe women are delicate ornaments rather than functional human beings. I reckon you've had a lucky escape, if you don't mind me saying so, miss?'

'I do mind!' Julia looked indignant. 'I happen to like a sensitive man.'

'Insensitive, you mean,' Lucie muttered. 'A woman is a very natural creature and she needs a man who accepts that she isn't always sweet and sunny but has her moods and a body that's at the mercy of old mother nature. Now Mr Rome likes women because they are women, not bits and pieces of Crown Derby to be put on a shelf in a nice arrangement.'

It was a remark Julia refused to find amusing, but for some odd reason she smiled over it as later on she made her way down the beach steps, the young gardener Tullio walking ahead of her carrying her picnic basket, a striped rug and several magazines.

The sun was hot and tawny like honey through glass, and the sea was littered with great globules of golden light, with silver trapped inside. Everything had a lazy air, and the meandering sands were patched gold and brown, the scattered rocks lapped by the water. Seabirds took languid swoops over the sea, their wings carved against the blue sky.

'What a perfect day!' Julia paused on the steps to take in the scene, her nostrils tensing to the wild scents of everything. Tullio turned to look at her, and she thought that with his torso bared to the sun and his black curly hair he looked like the wild god Pan. *Splashing and paddling with hoofs of a goat, and breaking the golden lilies afloat.* She smiled and his white teeth flashed in answer to her. In that moment she understood what Lucie had been getting at. Italian men more than most seemed to have an earthy reverence for all that was part of nature, and it was there in Tullio's dark eyes as they moved over her body. She could see his bold approval of her, a woman pregnant with an Italian baby.

He then said something in Italian, unaware that she understood his words. 'A pretty woman should not be alone on a beach but should have the company of a man.'

For an instant Julia was tempted to reply to him in Italian, and then decided that he might think she was inviting his company. It wasn't that she feared Rome's disapproval, it was her realisation that she felt rather lonely and would have liked to share her picnic lunch with someone friendly and uncomplicated. But it wouldn't do to invite the gardener to lunch. The others working in the villa wouldn't understand or approve, and she didn't want to hurt Maddalena's feelings.

When they reached the sands she politely thanked Tullio for carrying her basket and rug. 'I shall be fine just here. You go and have your own lunch.'

She saw the little expression of regret in his eyes, as if he had hoped that she might ask him to stay. 'Go along,' she smiled. 'Maddalena will be waiting to have lunch with you.'

'Sí, signora.' He inclined his curly head and the sun glinted on the religious medallion he wore. He and Rome were about the same age, she realised, but there was a worldliness about her husband that made him seem more mature than Tullio. It was probably his American upbringing and the kind of people he mixed with at the casino, and as she watched Tullio mount the steps in long strides she wondered if Rome would have been like him had he been born in Campania and taken to the soil for a living. She

tried to imagine Rome in such circumstances, but inevitably the image was obscured by the vivid reality of another ... Rome in a white dinner-jacket, wrenching loose his tie in reply to her accusation that he was a lowdown gambler. 'Right,' he said, 'let's see how you like being brought down to my level, my lady!'

Julia stood a moment staring at the sea beyond the arching groin of rock through which it swept back and forth in relentless motion, then shaking her head as if to clear it of images she laid her beach rug in a wedge of shade from the overhanging cliffs. She knelt and smoothed it out, feeling the little drag on her body where the baby lay curled inside her. A warmth stole over her skin, rising out of the neckline of the thin cream tunic she wore with a rust-coloured skirt which Lucie had altered.

Julia didn't want to think about Rome, but there was no chance of forgetting him the way she was. She would have liked to take a dip in the sea but could no longer get into her swimsuit ... unless of course she went in nude. A smile tugged at her lips and she glanced around her. The beach was entirely private to the villa and from here she couldn't be seen from the *terrazza* ... again she glanced at the sea and the longing to feel the creaming water on her limbs was too much for her.

Quickly she unzipped her skirt and stepped out of it, then removed her shirt and underwear. She gave her brassiere a wry look; it was two sizes larger than she normally wore and had been bought at the haberdashery in the village. Having a baby, she reflected, made a woman feel as if her body was being taken over by some lordly little creature who expanded it for his own use.

She stood there in the down-pouring sun and an almost sensuous feeling stirred through her body, and then she was running towards the sea, her hair bright and free about her bare shoulders. She ran into the sea from under the big groin of rock, gasping at the thrust of the water as it lifted her off her feet and turned her on her back, so that instinctively she opened her arms and moved her legs to the motion.

How good it felt! She was buoyant in the water, her body light and free again. She swam with smooth strokes, loving the silky coolness on her skin. Never in her life before had she swum without a suit, and now she understood why Rome never wore one.

She knew he didn't, having watched him in the pool unobserved, nothing on his body but the dark hair that lay like silk on his skin when he climbed out of the water and stretched himself on the sun-hot tiles. He would roll over lazily as the sun caressed every inch of him, just like a tawny tiger. 'Swim with me,' he had invited her, but she always refused, and he shrugged his shoulders as if it didn't really matter to him if she gave him her company or withheld it.

He knew there were other women who would welcome him in a pool, or in more intimate places. He had probably been aware since puberty that he had sensual appeal for women, and Julia knew that if it hadn't been for the baby it would have suited him to remain unmarried. He didn't have that air of wanting to be settled that some men had, and some nights he would prowl the garden court, a cigar glowing at his lips, and the following morning he would say at breakfast that he had to go to Naples. It was as if he felt caged up in the villa and needed the bright lights of the casino, the sound of the croupiers at the tables, the excited laughter of women who staked everything on the turn of a card or the spin of a ball on the roulette wheel.

It all went through Julia's mind as she swam until she was pleasantly gratified and ready for her lunch. When she came out of the water the sun was so warm that her body was dry before she reached her niche under the cliffs. She wrung the water from her hair and combed her fingers through its damp strands. Her hands travelled down over her neck and bosom, wiping off the salty bloom until her skin was supple and glowing.

She felt so good and couldn't confine her sense of freedom. The sensible brassiere was crammed out of sight in her raffia bag, and all she put on was her cream tunic which came to her thighs. She would wear her skirt later on when she returned to the villa.

She sat down on the rug and opened her lunch basket, which contained a salad, slices of cold chicken and ham, a wedge of cheese pasta, a crisp-looking pickle, fruit and a flask of creamy coffee. She sighed with contentment and tucked into the food, watching the sea as it creamed in and out of the big groin of rock.

The sands were resilient and soft as velvet between her toes, and as she licked pickle juice from her fingers Julia wished that time could stand still and the peace she felt could be suspended. She didn't want to think about the future and its problems; right now she wanted to pretend she was a teenager once again, sheltered and protected by her grandmother. How innocent and romantic she had been; she had truly believed that love could be as beautiful as the theme for Tristan and Isolde ... as the words that Romeo spoke to Juliet when she leaned from her balcony.

Julia lay on her rug, her slim legs stretched out so her feet were in the sand. Her senses were lulled by the sea sounds; a sensuous drowsiness was seeping through her body and the beach was hers, a great soft bed that cradled her and soothed her off to sleep. Her bright tousled hair lay spilled across the rug, her cheek rested on a curved arm, and the hem of her tunic revealed the slim honey smoothness of her legs. She looked vulnerable, lost in her dreams, unaware of the birds that came pecking the crumbs from her lonely lunch. The sea moved in its ceaseless motion, splashing the rocks and crooning to itself. Overhead the sky was cerulean shot with the gold of the sun, stroking warm across Julia's feet and winking in the green gem on her outflung left hand. Her fingers were partly buried in the sand, as if from the weight of the rings, the wide gold band that glistened richly, and the emerald which she had removed once or twice and been firmly told to replace.

A bird fluttered as in sleep Julia shifted her position as if to ease her own weight on the centre of her body. Then she settled into stillness again, and now her left hand lay against her body, lustrous green lights shifting in the emerald to the rise and fall of her breathing.

The air was filled with the tang of sea-wrack and ozone when she awoke, bemused and still half-dreaming. The sun was starting to go down and the sky was beautiful, unearthly, but all Julia was aware of was the male figure lounging on the sand above her reclining one. A cabana jacket lay unbuttoned against the brown firmness of his chest, open to the belt of his trousers.

A whiplash of fear curled through Julia's blood. Nerves fluttered in the pit of her stomach.

'W-what are you doing here?' The shafting sunset seemed to drain colour from her skin.

'My dear wife, you say the most amusing things.' His lips twisted into a smile and he touched her face before she could evade him. 'You have such poignant cheekbones and I can see the sunset in your eyes.'

Julia gazed up at him with the dilated eyes of her surprise at seeing him. 'When did you get back?'

'About an hour ago. I had a bite to eat, then I thought I'd come and say hullo to you.' His eyes slid down her figure. 'You were sleeping like a baby, so I waited until you awoke naturally. I've missed you, *cara mia*.'

'Really?' Julia felt herself go tense. 'I can't imagine that you went without feminine company while you were a whole week in Naples. It would go against the grain where you're concerned.'

'Would it?' He stroked a strand of hair behind her ear, where his fingers lingered, their tips against her earlobe. 'That goes to show how little you really know me.'

'I know you!' His touch was disturbing even though it was featherlight, but she wouldn't pull away from him in case he resorted to a more definite kind of caress. 'Even while you were away a woman was writing to you, no doubt a love letter as it was written on scented mauve paper. They can't leave you alone, can they?'

He smiled down at her, his teeth glimmering against his dark skin. 'Does it worry you, *mia*? Don't you like it that other women write to me, on scented mauve paper?'

'I couldn't care less!'

'Then why mention the subject?'

'For what it's worth, Rome, I am married to you and entitled to object to your *innamoratas* sending letters to the house I have to share with you. Couldn't she have written to the casino? Isn't that where you conduct your liaisons?'

'Take care, Julia.' He leaned closer, powerful and warm there in the flaming duskiness that was creeping over the beach. 'I came home in a congenial mood, hoping I might find that a week without my company had made you miss me. Haven't you missed me, even if only to fight with?'

'Why should I?' She defied his gaze, but couldn't ignore the looming strength of his shoulders. 'I—I told you before you left that I wish you'd stay away. Did you imagine I was being—provocative?'

'You're being very provocative right now, my dear.' And once again his eyes roved over her in the rumpled tunic ... her only covering. '*Santo Dio,* how fetching you look, half child and yet the woman who makes me a lovely child within that soft white body.'

A husky sensuality had come into his voice, and as the sunset burned out of the sky it seemed to leave its afterglow in Rome's eyes. 'I've got you now, haven't I, *mia*?'

'What do you mean?' Close like this to him Julia felt the vitality and power in his body, and she was made acutely aware of how alone they were in the gathering dusk of the beach.

'You aren't that innocent, my dear.' His lips were edged by a faintly mocking smile. 'I've been away for a week and I'd like you to welcome me home with a little more warmth.'

Julia debated with herself ... perhaps if she kissed him, he would then allow her to dress and they would leave the intimacy of the beach and return to the villa. She raised her face to his and could feel him watching her through half-lowered lashes. His strong arms slid around her and he drew her close to him, tucking her in against his chest, the hard hook of his legs enclosing hers, holding her imprisoned without hurting her. His mouth came down against hers. 'Kiss me, Julia,' he murmured.

She allowed her lips to touch the bold curve of his mouth.

'I shan't bite you, little fool. Put a bit more feeling into it!'

She felt the hammering of her heart in her rib-cage, and fighting a nervous urge to resist him she pressed her lips to his. 'There, are you satisfied?'

'No, I'm not.' He put his lips to the throb of a vein in

her neck and her breath quickened as she felt the stirring desire in his body.

'Rome—please——'

'I like it when you plead with me.'

'I—let me up!'

'Not yet, my sweet.' He leaned down until his face touched hers and his lips vibrated against her skin as he whispered something. Instantly she tried to struggle out of his arms, but they refused to release her and her movements only caused her tunic to ride up and reveal a little more of her bareness. She realised that if Rome was aroused she had only herself to blame for not being completely dressed, and even as she caught at his hair in an attempt to pull him away from her, she felt the tunic come open and his lips were against the curve of her breast. '*Santo Dio*,' he said huskily, 'I must have you, Julia. You can yell at the pitch of your lungs but no one will take any notice. I've given orders we aren't to be disturbed—do you hear me?'

'Don't hurt me——' She said it pleadingly.

'Hurt you?' His hand moved on her body and she gasped, but not with pain. 'Have I ever hurt you? You know the answer even if you won't admit it—ah, *mia*, you smell of the sea and you feel like satin—sweet satin doll, let me——'

His words died to incoherency, passion was released in him and there was no restraining it—it swept over both of them, and distant yet close Julia heard the sea as it came and went in the groin of rock.

Rome sat up staring at the sea, his hair black and tousled on his brow. He reached to his cabana jacket and drew his cigar-case from the pocket, along with his lighter. Julia lay and watched him as he lit a cigar and slowly released the rich smoke from his nostrils. His profile against the starlight was firm and bold, and his shoulders glistened, strong and supple, sloping down to a narrow waist and hips.

'A woman is like the sea,' he murmured. 'Not really conquerable, and just as unpredictable, with a mystery to her that a man never really discovers.'

'Does it provoke you, Rome, even though you're strong enough to make a woman do as you want?'

'Didn't you want it?' he asked moodily. 'At least you didn't plough my back with your fingernails, like the last time.'

Her gaze moved up and down his back and she remembered the smooth rippling of his skin over the muscles, the strange disinclination to claw at him. But it hadn't been like the last time. There had been no overriding urge to humble her ... he had held her in a different way ... there had been a tenderness in him, as if all the time he was thinking of the baby. Her fingers played absently with the sand. She was having his baby and he had wanted her because of that ... wanted the feel and touch and pleasure of the woman he had made pregnant. His fingers had traced the enriched curve of her breast and his lips had moved back and forth across their tender tips.

Julia tensed as within her a tiny foot seemed to kick her. 'Rome——' She bit her lip, and then knew she had to say the words. 'Give me your hand, Rome. The baby's moving!'

He sat there very still, and then he turned and she took his hand and guided it across her stomach to her side. She pressed his hand to her and a moment later felt the tremor that passed through him as the mysterious movement of his child was transmitted to him.

'*Amorevolezza*——' He stared down at Julia as the little movements died to stillness. 'Does it hurt you?'

She smiled a little and shook her head. 'It startles me

when it happens, but there isn't any pain. Now you know exactly what you've done to me, don't you, *signore*?'

He went on looking down at her, the black hair on his forehead, a brilliance to his grey eyes that defeated the darkness.

'Men don't really realise it, do they?' she said. 'Only women know there's more to it than——'

'Than what?' he murmured, when she hesitated.

'Pleasure.' She wanted to look away, but his eyes wouldn't let her.

'You were pleasured, *amata*?'

'Not—not when this happened.'

'But tonight?'

'Tonight—you were kinder.' She touched herself. 'Because I'm like this.'

'You like me when I'm kind, eh?'

'I'm only human, Rome.'

'Yes, by God.' He sighed deeply and his eyes went up and down her body in the tunic he had buttoned, unevenly. 'Come, we had best be getting home. The air is cooling down and I don't want you to catch a chill.'

'Because of the baby? I never imagined that your type of man could want fatherhood quite so much. Why, Rome? To spoil him and make up for what you didn't have yourself?'

'Why not?' He shrugged and drew her to her feet. She came only to his shoulder, and she felt the knowingness in her skin when his arm slid around her and he pressed the swell of her to him. 'Will you object if I make a fuss of my child?'

'I shan't be here to object,' she said quietly.

He said nothing in reply, his hand a firm pressure against her spine, until abruptly he let her go. She felt a coolness blowing up the beach on to her skin and turning away from him Julia found her skirt and stepped into it. She had expected anger but not acquiescence, and she closed the zip of her skirt with fingers that shook a little. Did she want him to argue the point just because she had lain in his arms so intimately? She knew that his main desire was centred in the child, and that for him this hour on the beach had been incidental to that desire. She supposed she was just being a woman, to whom a sensual experience had to have more meaning than a gratification of the body.

She glanced at Rome as he casually donned his jacket, the remainder of his cigar clenched in his teeth. It already seemed to her that their physical closeness had left no real impression on him, especially when he said: 'The sea air arouses the appetite. I had only a snack on my arrival home, now I'm ready for a hearty dinner. You must be hungry yourself, *mia*.'

'Not really,' she replied, shaking the sand grains from the rug and folding it. 'I had a good lunch.'

'But that was hours ago.' He took the rug and picked up the picnic basket. 'You'll be ready for your dinner once you've had a shower and changed into a pretty dress. Come, let's make tracks.'

They walked across the sands to the steps and they were halfway up when Julia had to pause to catch her breath. 'I have a stitch—it's all right, Rome. You have to remember that I'm carrying quite a little load inside me.'

'You shouldn't really use the beach when you have to climb up and down these steps—if anything happened——'

'Don't worry, Rome.' Her voice took a slight edge. 'I take very good care of your son and heir and do everything the obstetrician advises. He assures me that I'm carrying a very healthy and active baby. You felt that for yourself, didn't you?'

Rome's eyes flashed over her, for as always when she

stood in conjuction to him, his tall strong figure made her look fragile by comparison. 'Shall I carry you the rest of the way?'

'Of course not.' She started to climb again. 'I wouldn't want you to disable yourself. It would make your trips to Naples less entertaining for you.'

She heard him mutter an Italian cussword. 'Don't make insinuations you can't prove, Julia.'

She didn't reply, but when they reached the villa and were halfway across the hall she gestured at the table where several letters awaited his attention. 'Try the one in the mauve envelope,' she suggested.

He gave her a raking look, then strode to the table, dropped rug and basket to the floor and sorted among the letters for the mauve one. He glanced at the postmark before ripping open the envelope and taking out the folded sheets of notepaper. Julia watched as he skimmed the first few lines, then as he gave a soft laugh she made for the stairs and found as she mounted them that her legs were trembling. She felt a kind of fury ... as much with herself as with him. The soles of her feet inside her raffia sandals were gritty with sand, and she could hardly endure the mental image of herself in Rome's arms on the beach, her toes curling into the sand as the waves of sensual response lifted her on their crest, where she clung to rippling warm shoulders and was carried through troughs of unimaginable sensation.

Now she hated it for happening ... hated him who had made it happen. He was a master at it. Other women couldn't leave him alone once they'd been in his arms.

Julia flung herself on the bed and gripped the cover as if to tear it to ribbons. She'd make him suffer for laughing in front of her at the amorous words contained in another woman's letter!

'Had a good day, lovey?' Lucie had entered the room, carrying over her arm a flowered silk-chiffon dress she had altered for Julia; one of her New York dresses she was exceptionally fond of. Julia turned on her back and thought of the last time she had worn the dress. It had been at a cocktail party with Paul and he had said she looked flower-like, so cool and contained and not to be plucked by a careless hand.

'Did Mr Rome join you on the beach?' Lucie added.

Julia winced at the stabbing significance the words had for her. 'Yes,' she said, trying to thrust away those images whose torment was extra subtle because Rome shared them. She had responded to him, caressed him and sighed his name. He had made her react like other women who sought his arms in the velvety dusk of an Italian night.

'It must have come as a nice surprise.' Lucie gave her a careful look and Julia felt her skin grow heated, as if it showed that she had been in Rome's arms.

'It certainly came as a surprise.' Julia slid from the bed and combed her fingers through her hair. 'I'm all over sand and I need a shower. The *signore* is downstairs right now reading his letters, so I expect he'll be off again on another of his trips.'

'But he's only just got back.' Lucie stroked absently the silky fabric of the dress she held. 'Are you still at odds with him, Miss Julia? It could be that he has to get away from.'

'I daresay it helps,' said Julia, prodded to anger by the soft, affectionate way he had laughed as he read the letter from Spain. 'But you can't be so naïve, Lucie, that you don't know what really takes him to Naples—or wherever? *Amore* is second nature with men like Rome!'

'Aren't you at fault, miss, if you don't give him your love?'

'*My love?*' Julia gave a scornful toss of her head. 'You're letting your romantic imagination run away with you, Lucie. All he wants from me is this darned baby he forced on me—yes, forced! You flinch at the word, but you'd like even less the exact term for what Signor Demario accomplished at his casino in Naples. Had Grandma been alive she'd have made him pay for it!'

'Are you making him pay, Miss Julia?'

'I'm the one that's paying the piper!' Julia's green eyes flashed. 'Look at me—halfway up those beach steps I had to stop for breath like some obese senior citizen! I'm not like this because of love, Lucie. I'm like this because of——'

'Don't use that nasty word, miss.' Lucie laid the flowered dress across the bed stool and came to Julia. 'Come and have a nice bath and I'll loofah your back for you and wash your hair with avocado shampoo.'

'Don't try and soothe me as if I'm a child——' Julia broke off with a shaky sigh. 'I'm being a bit of a shrew, aren't I?'

'It isn't like you, lovey. You used to have a sweet nature.'

'That was before I grew up and found out that people can be cruel. I think Grandma was too sheltering of Verna and me. She should have allowed us to see how the children grew up in the back streets of New York, in those brownstone tenements. Maybe I'd be harder—like Rome.'

'Mr Rome isn't so hard, miss.'

'Lucie, you try my patience! I know him better than you, the way he can turn on the Latin ardour and make a woman believe she's the only one in all the world who matters to him. It's a fine art with his type—hot-natured, handsome, and about as capable of being faithful as a *cigale* in the corn. I've just had the pleasure of seeing him enjoy the contents of a letter from one of his *innamoratas*. A Spanish one, educated and rich from the look of her handwriting and the aroma of her perfume. I expect she sprayed it on the envelope to remind him of the last time they made love!'

'Miss Julia,' Lucie looked really shocked, 'how can you even think such a thing?'

'Easily. While reading the letter he laughed like a man with memories.' Julia turned and hastened into the bathroom. She wanted the shower pounding her skin, numbing her nerve ends, removing the feel of his lips and the touch of his hands. She flung off her clothes and stepped into the shower stall, taking with her a sponge and a large bar of Pears soap. She soaped and sponged all over, but there was one place she couldn't reach, and that was her mind.

It mocked her and unrolled each scene on its mini-screen, adding sound and broken scraps of dialogue.

Julia gave a choked little cry and pressed her hands to her ears. Rome had said such things to others and she couldn't bear it. Such endearments should be private, between two people, not shared with another woman who wrote to remind him of the occasions when he had held her in his arms. Had it been on a beach, a sky above filled with trembling stars, the sea in constant motion upon the rocks, moments torn out of time when the world stopped and heaven took its place?

Suddenly the shower was turned off and Lucie was wrapping a large towel around Julia and urging her out of the bathroom. She was rubbed dry like a child and a nightdress was slipped over her head. 'I'm putting you to bed, miss. You've had a little too much sun and sea air and you're overwrought. I'll ask Mr Rome if he'd like his supper up here with you.'

'I don't want him,' Julia said stubbornly. 'I was perfectly all right until he came home. He's the one who gets me all churned up a-and scared about everything. He unsettles me—you know he does.'

Lucie stroked a brush through Julia's damp hair. 'You fight him, miss, when it's much easier to give in.'

'But I didn't——' Julia bit her lip. 'We didn't exactly fight.'

'Then what's upsetting you?'

'That he—those other women. Like so much candy!'

'How do you know? How can you be sure? Why not give him the benefit of the doubt?'

'Scented letters!' Julia looked scornful. 'She's someone he knows—intimately.'

'An old flame, I daresay.' The long gliding brush strokes were making Julia's hair glisten in the lamplight. 'The *signore* is a mighty good-looking man and there would have been—flames.'

'They're still burning, Lucie. They aren't forgotten ashes.'

'If you didn't care for him, my lovey, you wouldn't be so churned up.'

'It's a matter of pride.'

'Pooh, pride.' Lucie waved it away with the brush. 'When you get to my age you realise there are more important things in life than letting your pride be a killjoy. Mr Rome wouldn't have come home feeling so lively if he'd been playing around with candy. D'you think I was born yesterday, miss?'

Julia flushed and twisted the rings on her hand. 'He's bigger than me, and with the baby hampering me I could hardly run away.'

'Yes, he's a fine figure of a man,' Lucie smiled. 'There, your hair looks very nice against that peach colour, and you've got quite a bit of colour in your cheeks. I'll go and fetch the *signore*.'

'You'll do no such thing,' Julia protested. 'I told you I didn't want him—let him stay downstairs and drool over his scented letter.'

'You know what he should do, miss.' Lucie smoothed the bedcovers. 'He should give your bottom a few spanks.'

'That would be good for the precious son and heir,' Julia scoffed.

'He's tucked away too nice and cosy to take harm from Mr Rome, whether he spanks you or canoodles with you. What you refuse to admit is that the *signore* has in his bones the marrow of kindness. I'm twice your age and I've worked as a maid since I was a bit of a girl, and you get to learn about people when you're in and out of their bedrooms. It isn't always the born rich who are the ladies and gentlemen. More often than not they're wilful and arrogant and about as generous as Scrooge. I've found out from Cosenza how good Mr Rome has been to the people hereabouts. Everyone likes him, and if you aren't careful, Miss Julia, he'll find someone else to console him—he's a big fine man and he has the needs of his nature, so you be warned in time.'

'And what is my wife being warned about?' Rome had strolled into the bedroom from the adjoining *salone*, and since coming up from the beach he had obviously taken a sauna and was clad in a white jacket, wine silk shirt and tie, and black trousers perfectly tailored to his lean hips and long legs. 'And what is more, *cara*, what are you doing in bed?'

'Lucie says I'm overwrought.' Julia felt his eyes skim the neckline of her nightdress and the contrast of her hair against the silk. Tiny nerves trembled under her skin, reacting to his vital darkness and boldly sculpted lips . . . those lips which only a short while ago had been so intimate with her.

A frown drew his brows together and he glanced at Lucie. 'There isn't anything amiss? I demand to know.'

Lucie smiled at him and shook her head. 'Miss Julia gets herself a little worked up—she was always a nervy one as a child and would sometimes cry over silly things and yet go to the dentist or put up with a bad cold as good as gold. I thought it would be nice, *signore*, if the two of you had supper up here.'

Still he frowned and gave Julia a searching look. 'That stitch in your side went away, didn't it?'

Julia gazed up at him and suddenly she knew a way to hurt him ... to keep him from touching her ever again. 'I do have a pain,' she said. 'I've had it ever since we came up from the beach.'

Rome caught his breath and Julia was almost startled to see how ashen he went around the nostrils, while the cleft seemed to sharpen at the centre of his chin. 'A pain?' he exclaimed, coming at once to the bedside, 'What is it—what's causing it?'

Her eyes met his and she saw from the look in them that each moment of their encounter on the beach was going through his mind. He had made love to her, therefore he had caused the pain which she claimed to be feeling!

'I must send for the doctor,' he said anxiously. 'We can't take any chances.'

Lucie had come to the bedside and was giving Julia a suspicious look. 'You said nothing to me about a pain, Miss Julia. Are you sure you have one?'

'Of course I'm sure.' Julia was looking at Rome and enjoying his discomfiture. 'As my husband says, we can't take any chances. He'd be so upset if I lost the baby——'

'Let me feel your forehead.' Lucie leaned over her and pressed a hand to her brow. 'Umm, you do feel a little feverish. Whereabouts is the pain?'

Julia indicated her pelvis, and as she did so she saw Rome's hands clench at his sides.

'I want the doctor to come and take a look at you, Julia. Is it very severe?'

'Bearable,' she said quietly. For the first time she had him at a disadvantage and she told herself she liked the feeling. Even so she turned her gaze away from his strained face. 'There's no need to send for the doctor, I expect it will go away. Perhaps I need something to eat.'

'Miss,' Lucie took her by the chin and looked into her eyes, 'has there been any bleeding?'

Julia heard Rome catch his breath and suddenly what had started as a game had taken a serious turn. 'No,' she said hastily. 'I—I think it's a hunger pain—I really do——'

'I'm fetching the doctor.' Rome strode to the door. 'I'll drive down myself, it will be quicker that way——'

'Rome, no!' Julia knelt up on the bed. 'I don't need him, really. You don't have to go driving down to the village at some breakneck speed—please! I'll be perfectly all right as soon as I've eaten my supper—I do get this gnawing feeling—it's because I'm eating for two. Please, don't go!'

He stood gripping the door handle, and then he swung round to face her. 'Are you playing a game with me?' His jaw was grimly set and there was a dangerous glitter in his eyes.

Julia huddled down into the bedclothes, feeling her mouth go dry. 'I—I expect I have indigestion——'

'Yes, something to gripe about.' His narrowed eyes raked over her, then he glanced at Lucie. 'Please leave us,' he said. 'I think I have to get to the bottom of this—infliction.'

'Yes, *signore*.' Lucie gave Julia a quick look, half-shaking her head as if to say that she was in for it, and deservedly so. Rome withdrew from the door as Lucie approached and he gave her a brief smile as she went out of the room, but as soon as he closed the door behind her, his smile was gone. He slid his hands into his jacket pockets as he came back to Julia, as if he didn't trust their inclination to give her a good shaking.

'I suppose you think you're clever?' he said, leaning over her and giving her the full benefit of the anger in his eyes. 'Well, I get the message, my dear, and you have my full assurance that what occurred down on the beach won't happen again. I have no inclination to touch a woman who stoops to petty spite in order to get even with a man, but for what it's worth, Julia, you weren't unwilling in my arms. You were as much a part of it as I was, and I wonder if that's why you had to pretend I'd hurt you in some way. *Santo Dio*, I felt as if the blood left my heart! But you'll never do that to me again—I wouldn't touch you now if you begged me to do so!'

Julia gazed up at him, her heart thudding so hard beneath the silk of her nightdress that she thought she might faint. The stiletto she had turned on him had now been reversed and it was as if a fine thread of pure steel was sliding in somewhere in the region of her ribs. She caught her breath at both the pain and the lean dark intensity of Rome's face in the lamplight. His eyes held that diamond brilliance, the pupils so enlarged they were like mirrors reflecting her white face. There wasn't a vestige of triumph left in her now ... she was feeling the backlash that spitefulness brought with it.

'Well, now we're even.' She turned her head away from him, her nerves shrinking when something landed on the bed with a thump.

'You can regard that as payment for all your recent suffering at my hands.' Never had he sounded more sarcastic. 'Take a look—I was told by the dealer that it's genuine Victorian, so it should suit your attitude very well, my dear.'

Julia didn't want to look at what he'd thrown on the bed,

but she knew he was in a smouldering rage that would intensify if she didn't show some interest in his gift. She felt the tremor in her hands when she opened the package and discovered a vanity-case of gold patterned with filigree and adorned by a glimmering pearl and a lustrous ruby set side by side.

'Purity and passion,' he mocked. 'I intended to buy you a trinket, but when I saw the box I couldn't resist it. The perfect gift for my pearl of a bride, eh? Does it appeal to you?'

'Yes, thank you.' She spoke tonelessly. 'The vanity-case is very nice.'

'And doubtless the woman who last used it was just as good at playing the shrinking violet.'

'Wouldn't it have suited your tempestuous *señorita*?' Julia flashed.

'I wouldn't dream of giving anything like that to Ramona Albañez.' He gave that soft laugh Julia had heard before in connection with the woman, and his casual mention of her name in their bedroom was a little too much for Julia's temper. One moment the vanity-case was in her hand and the next it was flying towards Rome and she saw it strike his cheek, making him flinch and step backwards, a livid mark showing against his skin. He gazed silently at her for about half a minute, then as if he no longer trusted himself he swung on his heel and strode out of the room, flinging the door shut behind him.

The gold box lay where it had fallen, half buried in the deep wool of the carpet. Julia crouched on the bed, appalled by what she had done. It could have struck his eye, and her stomach heaved as she pictured the blood and the agony. Suddenly she pressed a hand over her mouth and made urgently for the bathroom where she leaned over the toilet bowl and was wrenchingly sick. After several minutes she fell back against the tiled wall. Her body felt cold and yet there was a fine film of perspiration clinging to her skin.

Julia had never behaved in such a temperamental way in her life; such a wilful action could so easily have damaged one of Rome's eyes.

A sob caught in her throat and she sank down in the matting of the bathroom floor and buried her face in her hands. She could feel the tears seeping between her fingers and she felt almost as wretched as when she had found she was going to have a baby and the future had felt so frightening. She rocked back and forth in a kind of emotional agony, the tears running down her face and salting her lips. To-night she had satisfied the urge to hurt Rome, but in the process she had hurt herself as well, in a way so bewildering she hardly knew how to cope with it.

Rome had come to her from the beach, a seeking light in his eyes which she had quenched ... she had seen it flicker and die when he turned on his heel and left her, bearing on his face the bruise she had inflicted.

Lucie found her huddled on the floor and after bathing her eyes for her, helped her back into bed. 'I warned you, my lamb.' She stroked the tousled hair out of Julia's swollen eyes. 'When a man holds out the olive branch you don't knock it out of his hand. When you do that, it's a poor broken thing that you try to pick up again.'

Prophetic words, as Julia discovered in the days that followed and turned gradually into weeks.

CHAPTER SEVEN

THE *cigales* kept up a continuous chirring in the gullies of ilex and wild-growing oleander. A smouldering warmth lay over the sea which looked like beaten silver through the branches of the gnarled olive and pomegranite trees. There was a honey tang of sun-hot thyme and figs, and a whiff of citrus from the lemons whose branches shaded the little arbour at whose doorway was a winged Psyche of stone.

Julia no longer went down to the beach, for the climb back up the steps had become too much for her. Instead she came and sat in the cool arbour and read books or did some embroidery. Maddalena, proficient like most Italian girls at the art, had taught her how to do it and right now she was making a design of tarantella dancers on a night-dress-case. It kept her mind occupied, for having no close neighbours the villa was a quiet place whenever Rome was away from home.

Julia awaited the birth of their child in three weeks' time. She looked composed, with her hair worn for coolness at her nape, clad in the charming maternity dresses which had come from Naples. She kept well hidden the trepidation that she felt with each passing day. It wasn't the actual birth which she feared; it was her reaction to the moment when the baby looked at her and she found herself gazing into the velvety pupils and glimmering grey irises which she knew the child would inherit from the man she had sworn to leave ... who had accepted that she would leave when the baby was born.

Rome had told her she could go. 'I won't make you stay,'

he had said, a few days after they had quarrelled and she had flung the Victorian vanity-case at him. 'I don't want my child growing up in the kind of atmosphere you and I create. I shall love the little one enough for the two of us.'

Often Julia remembered the dignity with which he said it, and the way he looked, aloof and proud and never to be touched again, as she had touched his warm, tawny body as they passionately embraced on the starlit beach. He had withdrawn from any more contact with her; he was a polite, generous, kindly host, but he was no longer a husband.

Julia sighed, and then gave a gasp as the embroidery needle stabbed her hand. A shadow had fallen across the doorway of the arbour and when she glanced up a complete stranger was standing there, studying her, a drift of smoke from the thin dark cigar in his hand. He was of middle height, with heavy-lidded eyes and a dark moustache. He wore slacks and a Madras jacket, yet there was something of command in his attitude. His face held that tameless hint of danger she had often seen in Rome's. Like Rome's his face was somehow ancestral in its detailed Latin darkness ... as if he stood poised upon a chariot that was about to be driven at a dangerous pace. He had a hard chin but something of humour in the curve of his mouth.

'*Scusa, signora*, I startle you and you stab your hand. I hope it isn't too bad?'

'No——' Julia shook her head and wondered who he was.

As if guessing this he gave her a half-bow and drew his heels together. 'I must introduce myself, eh? I am Vitale Cantrelli, a good friend of your husband whom he may have mentioned to you?' A black eyebrow was raised enquiringly. 'This is so, *signora*? Rome has spoken of me to you?'

'Why—yes.' Julia remembered very well what Rome

had told her about this man, of Sicilian parentage born in America, who had been to prison while young and had been innocently connected with the death of Rome's father.

'You are Don Vitale,' she said quietly.

At once a humorous glimmer came into his dark eyes and he took a slow pull at his cigar. 'Do you mind?' he drawled, a slight American twang in his voice; the kind of sound Rome had deliberately eradicated from his own speech.

'I try not to judge people before meeting them,' she replied. 'Rome very much likes you, so why should I take the opposite view? I don't imagine that you have your henchmen with you.'

He laughed quietly, and she felt his eyes flick the softly flowered fabric of her dress. He was probably aware from Rome that she was soon to have a baby, and he said:

'I wouldn't want to make you nervous, *signora*. I understand there is a *neonato* shortly on the way. Rome is very happy about it, eh?'

Julia felt an inward quivering of nerves when he said that; Rome rarely spoke of his feelings these days. 'I expect so, *signore*. Latin men are very fond of children, aren't they? It's one of the nicest things about them.'

'Aren't there other nice things, *signora*?' He quizzed her through his cigar smoke and Julia couldn't help but catch the admiring gleam in his eyes as they stroked her hair. 'You must have thought so, being obviously espoused by a compatriot of mine.'

It occurred to Julia that he was curious about Rome's marriage and was perhaps wondering why he had taken an American girl for his wife when there were Latin women in pursuit of him.

'Rome didn't mention that you were paying a visit to Domani,' she said. 'He's in Naples right now and——'

'Yes, I know he's there on a transaction, but I understand

he'll be home very soon. He knew I might pay him a visit. Rome and I aren't formal about such things and I would have called sooner to be introduced to his wife, but for some time I've been in Spain—a personal matter that hasn't really resolved itself.' Don Vitale frowned and gazed up absently at the lemons clustering on the branches that arched over the arbour. 'Rome has found for himself a very attractive young woman to share his life. His fairly young life has held its tragedies, as you are no doubt aware? May I call you Julia? It's a Latin name, but a man has only to look at you to see you are very much the Anglo-Saxon type of woman.'

'Does it surprise you, Don Vitale, that Rome has married someone like me? As you've known him for a long time I expect you know more about him than I do.'

'He knew you as a child, did he not—Julia?'

'So he told you that?'

Don Vitale inclined his dark head and a glint came into his eyes. 'It's almost a modern variation of Romeo and Juliet, eh?'

'Their story ended tragically——' Julia gazed down at the half-completed dancers on the silk case she was sewing and took a grip on her composure. 'I've never been to Spain, but I've heard it's a very colourful country—that the women are particularly lovely.'

'Rome must take you there for a trip, I feel sure you'd enjoy the place and the people. The women have warm hearts and great loyalty and, indeed, lots of *sal*. I daresay Rome says the same of you, eh?'

Julia was lost for a reply, knowing as she did that Rome had lost interest in her as a woman and was only concerned that she give him the child she had said she didn't want.

'You've chosen a lovely day to visit Domani, *signore*.' She summoned up a smile. 'The summer seems endless in this part of Italy—oh, not that I'm complaining. I enjoy the warmth and the rich smells of everything.'

'This is a very charming region,' he agreed. 'Rome was fortunate to find a house here, but he seems to have a talent for making shrewd deals. What do you think of the one he has just made, eh?'

'I——' The question was unexpected. 'I wouldn't know anything about it. Rome doesn't discuss business with me.'

'No?' A black eyebrow was raised in some surprise. 'Yet I had the impression he had sold the casino and bought himself a fruit farm in Campania in order to be the respectable *contadino*. Surely he would only do that for your sake—yours and the *neonato*?'

'Has he really sold the casino?' Julia was gazing at Don Vitale in utter amazement.

'*Sí*. I have a certain interest in the deal and I can assure you he has made a very good profit. Negotiations started some time ago, and today he signs the papers that make him the grower of fruit instead of the gambler. I felt sure you must have influenced his decision.' A smile creased the hard brown cheek. 'I can't as yet imagine Rome as a son of the soil, not after seeing him so often at the casino, looking so suave in his white tuxedo, with such a keen grasp of the gaming business. Now he starts from scratch, and I wish him luck.'

Julia sat there twisting a silk thread around a finger. Instinct told her that Rome had cut loose from the gaming business for the sake of their child, making for himself a new way of life, a background more solid and secure than the environs of a gambling club. That he had gone ahead without telling her was further proof that he was excluding her from his life. He was giving her what she had asked for ... her freedom. All he desired in return was to care for their child of chance ... born out of furious words flung like dice across green baize, of emotions linked to their own childhood when she, a granddaughter of the grand house, was not allowed to play with the kitchen helper's son.

'Are you all right, *signora*?' Don Vitale had entered the arbour and was leaning over her in some concern. 'You have gone very pale and I can see you are trembling—the child is due when?'

'It—isn't that. Your news about the casino has taken me by surprise. I had no idea, you see, that Rome had decided to sell and start anew in something else.'

'Perhaps I should not have mentioned it. Maybe he was saving up the news for you, but I took it for granted——' There he broke off as from among the trees his name was called.

'Vitale, where are you, *querido*?'

'I am here, *carissima*.' He stepped again to the entrance as a slender female figure appeared in the little clearing where the arbour was situated. Don Vitale held out a hand to the woman who came instantly to him, sliding her elegant hand into his. They smiled at each other, and Julia watched them and decided instantly they were deeply in love.

'*Querido*,' the woman said eagerly, 'if only we might find a house like this! I have been exploring and it has such charm, such tranquillity here above its own beach. Other people can't intrude unless one invites them! Ah, Vitale, could we ever live like this? Dare I hope——?'

He carried the slim hand to his lips and kissed the back of it, the fingertips, and then last of all the palm where his mouth lingered. 'If you have the courage, *carissima*. If you have the trust in me that your family lacks. That is why I brought you here, to visit my good friend Rome and his young wife. Come, meet her!'

He drew the woman into the arbour and Julia felt an

instant admiration and response to someone unusually beautiful. Her hair was blue-black and held away from her detailed Latin face by a pair of tortoiseshell combs. Her skin was smoothly olive, closely moulded over high cheekbones; her full mouth was a deep scarlet and her eyes were the dense mauve of tulips, the kind they called black tulips.

'May I present to you, *signora*, the Señorita Ramona Albañez de los Reyes, who has the gracious kindness to be my *fidanzata*.'

To say that the introduction took Julia's breath away would be putting it mildly. All she could do for several moments was to gaze at Romano Albañez in total astonishment... so this was the woman who had written to Rome! Had she, upon finding him married, then turned to Don Vitale for consolation?

'I—I'm pleased to meet you, *señorita*,' she managed to say.

'I have often wondered,' white teeth gleamed against the deep red lips, 'just how she would look, the girl who married the so handsome Rome, and now I see for myself that you are as fair as he is dark. I long to see you together. Will I have that pleasure?'

'I don't really know.' Julia felt bewildered, for the beautiful Spanish woman gave no sign that she had ever been romantically involved with Rome. Her fingers were entwined with Don Vitale's and she had a vulnerable look about her despite the elegance of her silk suit, her poise and obvious culture. She seemed to incline towards him, as if his solid strength was as necessary to her as the air she breathed.

'Rome comes and goes on business,' Julia explained, 'and I can but hope that he's coming home today. I'm sure he'd be disappointed to miss you.'

'My disappointment would be equal,' Ramona smiled,

and glanced at her fiancé, moving her arm so that a wide gold bracelet gleamed against her wrist; the traditional engagement symbol for a Spanish woman. 'It was upon Rome's good advice that Vitale and I became betrothed. My—my family was opposing this, but Rome wrote back to say that I must allow no one, not anything, to stand between us. That I must be cruel if there was no other way. That hearts could bleed but also heal, if the roots of love were strong enough. I was brought up very strictly, you understand. Another man had been chosen for me, but I have loved Vitale for three years and I could no longer bear to be apart from him. I expect you understand?'

The densely mauve eyes dwelt fleetingly on Julia's body, obviously burdened by Rome's baby; the outward sign to other people that a mutual loving passion had been responsible for the condition. As always Julia blushed slightly when people looked at her in that way, as if they pictured her in the passionate arms of her husband. Those arms she had imagined around Ramona Albañez, who now revealed that she had loved for years the Sicilian whose path had crossed Rome's so fatally a long time ago, forging between them a strange kind of friendship.

Julia's gaze dwelt on Don Vitale, a man who was unacceptable to Ramona's family yet who had a physical dynamism that would make it hard for a woman to forget him.

Pressed by her family to forget him, she had written to Rome, his friend, who had replied that love was worth its hurts, and even its cruelties.

'So,' Don Vitale snapped his fingers at the air, 'Ramona's family is a noble one and I am nothing in their eyes, but we are everything to each other and that has to count for something, eh? I asked for marriage, was adamantly refused, and so at Rome's suggestion we come here *fuga*—we elope, you understand, and will be married here in Campania.'

'Oh, Vitale,' Ramona clutched his arm and gazed at him with anxious eyes, 'if only they could understand my feelings and accept you! I am hurt for you—you are so good to me, kinder than anyone, more loving than a woman dreams of. I couldn't give you up. Rome said the same. He knows your true self, as I do.'

'So now you are begining to trust that it will work?' he smiled. 'How come?'

Her answering smile was shy. 'I know that I want your baby,' she said simply. 'I want what Julia has—it is the realisation of being a woman and nothing else counts beside it.'

He glanced at Julia, his eyes narrowed. 'Would you agree with that, *signora*?' he asked. 'Do you think a man has the right to take a woman away from all that she is accustomed to; her family and friends, her way of life? Has it made you happy?'

'How could Julia not be happy?' Ramona exclaimed. 'Married to a man like Rome, living here in this charming villa above the sea, and soon to hold his child in her arms? It is a love story come true, is it not?'

Julia felt as if something stabbed into her side, then slowly twisted. 'Shall we go to the house and have tea?' She gathered her embroidery silks together and bundled them into her raffia workbag. 'I—I'm longing for a cup. Aren't you, *señorita*?'

'Please to call me Ramona. I already feel that we are friends and if I persuade Vitale to buy a house in Campania we shall see each other often—we have in common that we both love Italian men, eh?'

Julia summoned a strained smile to her lips but didn't dare to meet the perceptive dark eyes of Don Vitale. 'The people of Campania are terribly nice and I do hope you find a house. According to Rome this one was quite run down at the time he bought it, but as you have seen, he has gradually restored it and modernised some of the interior. I—I must show you the nursery, Ramona. There are toys enough to keep three or four children amused.'

'Perhaps Rome is planning for that,' Ramona smiled. 'Italian men have a charming way with children, have they not? They can play with them, but Spaniards are more dignified and they like to treat their children as young adults. I had only one brother who was older than myself and my own childhood was a very sedate one, and I felt compelled to obey my father's every wish—until I met Vitale. It was in Venice where I was staying with a convent friend and her family.'

She glanced at him, her body gracefully inclining towards him, almost as if he were a ray of warmth that drew her to him. 'I was exploring with my friend when I went astray in one of the old *palazzo* courts and lost my way. It was getting rather dark and I was becoming very nervous when I ran into Vitale. I thought,' she laughed, 'that he looked such a brigand with that black moustache, but almost at the first meeting of our eyes there was a kind of—how does one explain it? A flash of instinct, of revelation, as if we had met before in some former life. You must know what I mean, Julia. It must have happened with you and Rome.'

'I first knew Rome when I was a child,' Julia replied. 'Come along, I'm gasping for a cup of tea.'

'Allow me, *signora*.' Don Vitale assisted her to her feet and she knew at once that he felt her trembling. She braved his eyes and smiled slightly.

'I am all right, *signore*. I get a little fatigued, that's all, and after we've had some tea my maid Lucie will insist that I take a rest. You and Ramona might like to swim in the pool, or go down to the beach. I have a suit that Ramona can wear, and I'm sure a pair of Rome's briefs should fit you.'

'Certainly you must take your rest, Julia, and be assured that Ramona and I will manage to amuse each other for an hour or two. Is that not so, *carissima*?'

Ramona laughed softly in answer, as if being alone with him was the most exclusive delight of her life. Julia could only hope for Ramona's sake that the strong love she felt for Vitale would guard her against the perils of his profession, and as they made their way into the *salotto* for tea, Julia felt a sudden sense of relief that Rome had never been drawn into the Don's organisation even though he had mixed socially with some of its colourful characters.

It had left him free to sell the casino and start afresh, but the Don was committed and Ramona had to be aware of that, even if it didn't show in her manner. There was certainly nothing *brutto* about him, and whenever he looked at Ramona there was a grave kind of tenderness in his eyes. She was his angel even if she did not know that he had sold his soul to the devil.

They had tea and toasted cakes with butter, and then Julia excused herself for a couple of hours. 'I'll just show you the nursery before going to my room,' she said, and left the pair of them in there, standing arm in arm and obviously locked in mutual dreams of a family of their own. Julia felt a stab of envy; it had to be a kind of bliss to be so certain that you loved . . . and were loved.

Lucie helped her out of her dress and she slid into bed with a little sigh. The blinds were drawn so the silvery room took on an air of peace and quiet.

'All right, my lamb?' Lucie stroked a hand across Julia's brow. 'No aches or pains that you shouldn't have?'

'I'm just a little tired. If Don Vitale and his fiancée want to go swimming, will you see about a pair of suits for them?'

Lucie nodded. 'She's very beautiful, but he gives me the shivers. Cosenza was telling me——'

'I know what she's told you.' Julia frowned slightly. 'It's true, of course, but I think he keeps that side of his life well away from Señorita Albañez. He's quite the gentleman, really.'

'I won't be sorry to see Mr Rome back home. Are they staying overnight?'

'I expect so. You'd best tell Cosenza to prepare dinner for four, just in case Rome is on his way home. Lucie, he's sold the casino and bought a fruit farm here in Campania.'

'Well, I never! You must be feeling pleased about that, Miss Julia.'

'He never said a word about it to me. He obviously thought I wouldn't be interested—you do know, Lucie, that we're separating after the baby is born?'

'I know that's what you have in mind, but I don't see how you're going to bring yourself to do it, miss. Your heart isn't hard enough for that, and you'll break it if you walk out on your own baby. Besides, what is there for you to go back to? You're better off with Mr Rome——'

'He doesn't love me. He married me to give the baby his name.'

'You have his name as well, miss. You have your rights, and you can't tell me he's the sort of man hard enough to throw a woman out of her child's life. You can't tell me that, Miss Julia!'

'No, I'm not telling you that.' Julia smiled slightly, for Lucie's vibrant hair always seemed to crackle when she was aroused. 'You don't have to defend his principles to me, but when a man and a woman live together and the atmosphere between them is one of disharmony, then you know it isn't good for a child. Rome has made up his mind that his child is going to have a happier time than he had himself as a boy, and I don't fit into his future plans. I have my pride, Lucie. I can't stay at Domani if I'm not wanted, and I daren't let the baby get used to me. I—I have to leave before that happens.'

Julia broke off, for her voice was breaking up and she had to fight again for composure; she had to make herself go on with what she had to say.

'Lucie, I want your promise that you'll stay at Domani in my place a-and be as good to my baby as you've always been to me. Will you promise?'

'Oh, miss——'

'Please, Lucie! Rome will agree to it if I ask him to let you be the baby's nurse. He likes and trusts you, a-and when I go away, I shall go knowing that my son or daughter is in good hands—hands that will guide and love and care for my baby.'

'Oh, my lamb, I can't bear you to talk about going away!' Lucie sat down on the bedside and rocked Julia in her arms as if she were a child again. 'I won't let it come to that—I'll speak to Mr Rome——'

'No, Lucie! You'll do no such thing! I forbid you to go begging to him—my God, it would be like something out of *East Lynne*! He married me because he had to, and I have to honour the debt and set him free when the time comes.'

'Lots of couples marry because they have to, miss.'

'We weren't in love. I told you what happened, Lucie.'

'Are you going to hold it against him all his days, miss?'

'I—I'm not being vindictive.' Julia looked shocked. 'I just can't live with him the way things are—I have to find the courage to leave, and I think I'll be brave enough if I know you're here and taking care of the baby. If I don't see it or hold it or anything like that——' All at once Julia was crying, and it took some time before Lucie soothed her. Exhausted by her tears, she fell asleep, her fair hair tousled on the pillow, something haunting her face that held Lucie at the bedside for long and silent minutes. Then with a sigh she drew the silk coverlet closer over the young burdened figure and withdrew quietly from the room. She had the look of a woman who was extremely worried.

Moonlight silvered the *terrazza* and three of the occupants lounged in the cane easy chairs while Don Vitale stood by the parapet, a glass of wine in his hand.

'Alla salute!' He raised the glass to Rome and then to Julia. 'You certainly chose well when you bought this place, *compare*. On a night such as this you have the moon to yourselves, no?'

Rome slowly smiled and drew on his thin Italian cigar. He had arrived home just in time for dinner, so he and Julia had not exchanged more than a few words of greeting. He was looking fit but a little tired, she thought, but now he seemed more relaxed as she guardedly watched him through her lashes, always prepared of late to glance swiftly away if he should look at her. Before coming down to dine she had carefully bathed away all traces of her tears, and as an extra precaution had applied smoky-green colouring to her eyelids. She wore a full-skirted lace dress almost the same colour, and her hair was swathed to the crown of her head, leaving her neck slender and bare except for a thin gold chain with a little cross attached.

'I adore your house, *caro*.' Ramona was moving a silk fan slowly back and forth, and woven into the silk were menacing peacock eyes that moved to the movement of her hand. 'If I lived in such a place I would never want to go elsewhere. You have all that is needed on your threshold, the sea washing the beach, your wooded garden to walk in, that quaint village with its little shops, and a nursery that waits for your *bambino*. Julia was good enough to show us, but I imagine that for the first few weeks you will allow the little one to sleep in its cot in your own bedroom. If I had a baby I couldn't bear to be separated from it, not for a minute.'

Silence gathered and Julia could feel the fingers of her right hand grinding into her left one the rings that she wore. A gust of cigar smoke hovered and drifted from Rome's direction, and then her heart lurched as his eyes caught at hers before she could look away. His gaze was so penetrating that it seemed to reach down inside her, and again she felt as if something twisted in her body and her teeth bit down on her lower lip.

'Julia is an American,' he said. 'They have a less sentimental view of these matters.'

'But anyone can see that Julia is a woman of feeling.' Ramona reached across and pressed her hand. '*Madre di Gesu*, but your hand is icy! Are you cold on such a warm night?'

'I—I'm always naturally cool——' Julia swallowed and reached to the cane table for her wine, half-wondering if Rome would make some sardonic comment.

'I do like your dress,' she said quickly to Ramona; it was of supple silk, the bodice casually draped, the long skirt patterned with big black dahlias. 'Did you buy it in Madrid? I've heard the shops are very good there.'

'Yes, Madrid. I spoil myself and have my own dressmaker there.' Ramona moved her eyes over Julia. 'I admire the way you keep yourself attractive; some women don't bother at all when they are pregnant, as if the husband ceases to matter for a while. You obviously wish for Rome always to find your company sweet and nice. I hope, Rome, that you appreciate the effort from a wife heavy with child?'

'Of course I do.' His eyes were upon Julia as she drank from her wine glass, and felt as if hot little wires were being pulled through her collarbones and down through her rib-cage. She was full of odd little feelings these days and could only connect them with her condition.

'I think Julia must know that, at least,' he added. 'It's in her nature to be *chic*, and I remember that even as a child she always looked as nice and neat as a sprig of lemon, her long hair in a ribbon and shining like lemon fruit. Upon one occasion I was a bad boy and dropped strawberry ice-cream all over her shoes—I made her cry.'

'You wicked devil!' Ramona gave him a rap on the wrist with her fan. 'I was telling Julia earlier today that I longed to see the two of you together. You are so opposite in colouring that I wonder who the baby will resemble.'

'Rome,' Julia said quietly. 'Darkness is more dominant than fairness.'

'But what of the eyes?' Ramona exclaimed. 'Yours are green and Rome's are grey, and I predict that your child will have eyes that combine those two colours. Don't the two of you find it exciting wondering what this new little personality will be like and how he or she will grow up?'

This time that stab and twist feeling was so distinct in her body that Julia couldn't suppress a gasp.

'Is anything wrong?' Rome demanded, as if he were keyed in to her reactions.

'Just funny little sensations.' She leaned back carefully in her armchair. 'I believe your baby, Rome, is becoming impatient to see what kind of a world we live in.'

'It has its perfect moments.' Ramona was gazing at the sky. 'That great moon makes me feel very mortal, and yet I believe that life has no mortality between people who are truly in love. Or am I an incurable romantic?'

'Women react to the moon, and moonlight certainly becomes women.' Rome had risen from his chair as if suddenly he felt restive. He moved across to the parapet where Vitale was standing and gazed down at the sea, his profile etched fine and strong against the moolit sky. The sea and the beach held his gaze for several minutes, until abruptly he turned his back on them.

'Love is a revelation and no man has to be a saint to experience it.' Don Vitale held his cigar halfway to his lips and his smile didn't quite hide the menace in his nature. 'A man must give thanks when the arrow hits him square in the solar plexus. I know I do!'

'You speak, *querido,* as if this arrow of love only attacks men,' said Ramona, her fan poised against her lips.

'Women are love; they are the embodiment of it, like salt on the table and sugar in the jam.' He strolled across the *terrazza* to her and leaned down to kiss her cheek. He caught Julia's gaze and winked at her. 'When a Spanish woman places the fan at her lips she's inviting herself to be kissed. These women are quite flirtatious, you know, in their subtle way.'

'What would you do, Vitale, if I flirted with other men?' Ramona asked him, stroking her fan against his hardened cheek.

'I might take your lovely neck in my hands and snap it in half.' His fingers touched her necklace of black pearls from which was suspended a milky pearl heart. His fingers locked about the gem and Julia had the feeling that Ramona's living heart was held just as securely in Vitale's strong hand.

'Latin men are such ruthless lovers,' Ramona smiled, 'and only a foolish woman would want it otherwise. Don't you agree with me, Julia?'

'I agree that they're ruthless,' she replied, and without glancing at Rome she was aware of him leaning with dark grace against the parapet that jutted above the beach where the sea tossed back and forth on the shingle. There on a night like this one she had seen the moon turn to fire in his eyes when he made her surrender to him . . . afterwards she had said things that turned the glow to grey ashes.

'Ruthless and yet romantic,' Ramona murmured. '*Saudade*, we call it; an awareness that no matter how physically close we might get to another human being, we are never going to know completely what that person is feeling and thinking. When we love we are as helpless as stars that might fall out of heaven at any moment. Rather fearful in a way.'

'But also exciting, *carissima*.' Vitale touched the gold bracelet on Ramona's arm. 'In a few days' time we shall be married, and if you fall at any time, I shall be there to catch you.'

'Yes.' She met his dark eyes and caught her breath audibly at what she saw in them. 'You will be there, *querido*.'

He nodded his reassurance, and then turned to look at Rome. 'We are grateful to you, *compare*, for saying we might stay at Domani until the wedding, though it goes without saying that I shall stay in the village the night before the ceremony.'

'If only my family were going to be there,' Ramona sighed.

'It has to be me or your family, *carissima*. We have discussed this so often, so be very sure——'

'I am very sure that I love you, Vitale.' Ramona spoke with a deep, warm fervency. 'If I can't be with you, then I'm not really living. You—you alone matter beyond anything, and I say this in front of Julia and Rome because they must feel the same way about each other. Unless one lives with the person one loves, then life has no real meaning. I wanted my family to accept you, but if they can't then it is better to have friends who bring no doubts but only good feeling to our wedding.'

She turned to Julia and reached out to touch her hand. 'You will be well enough to attend, *cara*?'

'Of course,' Julia smiled. 'I wouldn't miss your wedding for anything, and I'm assured by my doctor that the baby isn't due until a fortnight after the ceremony. I know I look huge, but——'

'You look charming,' Ramona said quickly. 'As Rome is to be Vitale's best man, then I wish you to give me away.'

'Like this?' Julia smiled uncertainly, and then found herself looking at Rome for his reaction. He was frowning slightly, as if the idea didn't really appeal to him.

'What do you think, Rome?' she asked. 'Would you mind?'

'I'm agreeable if it won't be a strain on you, Julia,' he said, a little to her surprise. She had thought that he didn't like the idea of her being on show in front of the congregation; a wedding in the village church was bound to attract people, and Vitale was arranging that the local inn lay on a spread of food, with the traditional roasted pig. The villagers loved a party and they'd flock to the event.

'I'm sure I shall be all right,' she said. 'Everyone knows about the baby, so I shan't feel too conspicuous.'

'Then by all means give Ramona away, but I'm going to insist that you return home early from the party. I forbid any undue risk at this stage, Julia.'

'Of course,' she said, and refrained from adding in front of company that she knew he was concerned for the child and not for her. She didn't wish to disillusion Ramona, who took it for granted that she and Rome were madly in love and expecting a child who was the result of their passion for each other.

'Have you decided where you're going for a honeymoon?' she asked Ramona.

'We are going to Venice where we met three years ago. Vitale has booked us a suite in a lovely old *palazzo* and we shall do all the romantic things, such as holding hands in a gondola as it glides along the canals.'

'Which, my sweet,' Vitale drawled, 'are never too salubrious.'

'What if they aren't?' she chided him. 'People on honeymoon should only be aware of each other, and I shall expect your exclusive attention day and night.'

'I promise to give it, *carissima*.' His smile was slightly wicked, and he stood watching as in something of confusion Ramona opened her silk fan and fluttered it against her flushed cheeks.

'Don't look at me like that,' she pleaded. 'Not until the good *cura* gives you permission to do so!'

He laughed quietly, and all at once Julia felt rather depressed and decided it was time for her to retire to her room. She edged forward in her chair as she prepared to rise rather cumbersomely to her feet, and in a stride Rome was suddenly there and her hands were gripped strongly as he raised her to her feet. Her gaze lifted to his face, but it was courteous and unreadable.

'We are going to leave you lovebirds alone in the moonlight,' he said, sharing a glance between Ramona and Vitale. 'You know where your rooms are, and if you wish for anything at all my man Giovanni will be of immediate service. May you both rest in peace under my roof.'

'*Mille gracias*, Rome.' Ramona extended a hand to Vitale, who took it at once. 'You cannot imagine how grateful we are to you and Julia. It's so good to have such kind friends.'

'I'm glad we're friends.' As Julia spoke she felt Rome slide an arm around her and press his hand against the fullness of her waist, a protective gesture, she knew, rather than a loving one.

'Being here at Domani will always be a warm memory for us. Ramona drew Vitale's hand to her cheek. 'Love is such a precious emotion and when two people bring it to life between them, then they must guard it like a flame from the wind. They must nourish it with tolerance and tenderness. Always remember, Rome, that women are vulnerable and that life is more merciless towards them. Very soon Julia will undergo an experience that you may only imagine, so try to share her pain as you have shared her pleasure.'

Rome inclined his head. '*Buona notte*, my friends.'

He walked with Julia to the staircase, still holding his arm around her. At the foot of the stairs she attempted to disengage herself. 'I'll be all right, Rome.'

'I'll come up with you,' he said firmly.

'We haven't an audience now, Rome.' The words were out of her mouth before she could stop them. 'You no longer have to impress anybody with a show of concern for me.'

'Nor you with a show of sweetness,' he rejoined, 'but all the same I'll come with you. You are looking tired.' His arm remained in its firm position about her body as they mounted the stairs. 'Are you quite sure you want to give Ramona away at the wedding, Julia? Don't agree to it just to please her. She can be very beguiling, but she'll understand if you don't really want to do it.'

'I'd like to, if you don't think I'll look too conspicuous.'

'I'm concerned for your well-being,' he replied.

'Rome,' a hint of tiredness crept into Julia's voice, 'don't you mean that you're concerned that I do nothing to risk the well-being of the baby? I hope to God nothing goes wrong, because you'll be bound to blame me! I showed Ramona the nursery and she was amazed by all those toys.

I could tell what she was thinking, that it doesn't always do to want something with all your heart. I—I've seen you watching every step I take. You drum it into Lucie to make sure I rest each day. You give orders to Cosenza about the food I should eat. I hate yoghourt and often feel more like eating sausages or ice-cream.'

'Strawberry?' he murmured, a quizzical gleam in his eyes as they met hers. When they paused at the bedroom door, he touched a finger to the crescents of shadow beneath her eyes. 'Don't think I have no concern for you, Julia. I am daily aware of what you are going to face and you have seemed very tense this evening. Would you like me to stay with you tonight?'

Her eyes widened and her surprise mingled with a certain longing, which she instantly suppressed. 'No, I shall be fine,' she said coolly.

'Don't be foolish, Julia. I'm not a boor who is asking for your body—as if I would! But the nights can seem long and the things we fear seem to come closer to us in the darkness. You are soon to have my child and I wish to be of some help to you. Don't shut me out of something we both have a share in.'

'I'm not afraid of the pain,' she said. 'The pleasure was yours——'

'That isn't the whole truth, my dear. It never was.'

'How do you know what my feelings were?'

'Because you were in my arms and when a man holds a woman that close he feels her reactions as he feels his own. *Santo Dio*, why do you persist in denying that when we made the baby we had a mutual joy from it!'

'Don't—how can you say that? We were strangers after all those years and you speak as if—as if that night in Naples was a kind of romantic reunion a-and nothing could have stopped what happened. You want to ease your conscience because the real truth is that you wanted to punish a Van Holden for the hard times your mother had to face. That's the reality, Rome, not the fiction you've dreamed up for yourself. When I left the casino that morning I felt like a tramp as I walked along the seafront. I felt as if it showed that I'd been in your arms the entire night—a man who promised he'd make me feel cheap!'

'Not cheap,' he said grimly. 'You go too far, Julia!'

'I felt so ashamed, so low, my pride was crawling along the ground!'

He gazed down at her, his jaw set and hard, the cleft deeply shadowed at its centre. 'I never meant to make you feel like that. I let you leave the casino alone because that was what you wanted——'

'Wasn't it a little late to give me what I wanted, Rome? Couldn't you have done that before we had to end up married to each other?'

'I take it you prefer to be alone tonight?' He removed his arm from around her and thrust his hands into his pockets.

'Yes.' Her face was a quiet mask of pride. 'I won't give you the satisfaction of helping me through the next twenty-one days. I can do it alone. It's good practice for when I leave here—alone. I know you won't let me take the baby with me.'

'No.' His face was adamant. 'The child belongs here at Domani with me!'

'At least I know where I stand.' Julia opened the bedroom door. 'I'd like you to allow Lucie to stay and be the baby's nurse. You won't find a better or kinder nurse and I'll know the baby is in good hands.'

'I'd like that as well.' His face and voice were devoid of expression. 'I hoped we could be friends——'

'Friends?' She smiled at the idea. 'Even when we were

children we couldn't be—I used to think it was my grandmother's over-protectiveness where Verna and I were concerned, but it's something else that gets in the way—something without a name. I used to be aware of it when we were young. Speaking to other children was easy, but when I looked at you I felt tongue-tied. When I did try to break down whatever it was between us, you glared at me with your grey eyes and flung my offering all over my shoes. I thought I cried over the shoes, but I know now that I cried because I felt hurt. Goodnight, Rome.'

She entered the bedroom and closed the door on his tall darkness and brooding face. Tiredly she leaned her shoulders against the door and felt an ache low down in her back. As she rubbed the ache with her hand, tears glittered in her eyes. She had chosen to be alone, but the night ahead stretched into a darkness where something waited, patient and sinister, so that she hastily put on the lights and glanced around the big, silvery room. All was quiet and reposeful, yet she shivered as she stood at the dressing-mirror and unpinned her hair, which fell in glimmering fairness about her shoulders.

The feeling persisted that a dark shadow stood waiting behind her, and with a gasp she tugged at the bell-pull that would bring Lucie to her.

When Lucie came into the room she was carrying a small tray with a dish on it and there was a glimmer of pinkness through the glass container on the dish.

'Mr Rome came to the kitchen and said you might fancy some ice-cream, so I've brought you some.'

Julia felt the tip of her tongue move involuntarily around her lips. 'My throat is rather dry,' she said huskily.

'Then hop into bed and have it there,' Lucie smiled. 'It's strawberry ice-cream.'

A reluctant smile tugged at Julia's lips. What was it

about Rome that had always eluded her, as if she knew him almost as she knew herself, and the next instant didn't know him at all?

'The *signore* did say as well that you'd probably enjoy some fried sausages, but we don't want you awake half the night with indigestion, do we?'

Julia gave a slight laugh. The bedroom felt warm again and for now the dark shadow had retreated into its hiding place. Installed in bed with her ice-cream she looked, Lucie said, just like a small girl again enjoying a clandestine treat.

'Some small girl,' Julia scoffed, patting her stomach. 'I hope the little devil is enjoying the treat. While we were sitting on the *terrazza* he gave such a turn inside me I thought I'd faint.'

'What sort of a turn?' Lucie looked concerned. 'A painful one?'

'An impatient one. He's tired of me and wants his father.' Julia kept her gaze lowered as she finished the ice-cream. 'Rome wants you to stay on as nurse, Lucie. I hope you will.'

'We'll discuss it when the time comes, Miss Julia.' Lucie took the empty dish. 'You won't be able to give that baby up, not if I know you.'

'Rome won't give him up—he's already said so.'

'What an obstinate pair you are! The little mite isn't born yet, and already he's a tug-of-love baby.'

Julia winced and slid down carefully in the big bed, as wide as it was long and meant to be shared by someone else. She drew the silky covers to her chin and allowed the physical weariness to creep over her. She didn't want to think about tomorrow, she wanted to dream tonight that she was safe in strong arms and loved as she knew somewhere in her soul it was possible to be loved. She could smile now at the tepid emotions she had shared with Paul

Wineman; she had grown up since those days and sensed that love could be powerfully divine ... if only she could reach it. She felt sometimes that it was there beyond her dreams, so that waking one day she might find that the dream had turned into a reality.

'Sleep fast, my lamb.' Lucie touched her slightly hollowed cheek.

'Lucie,' she murmured, 'do you think dreams ever come true?'

'If they're meant to, though if you depend on dreams for your happiness you're going to find them a lot less substantial than real life. You have to ask yourself if the dream is nicer than what you really have.'

'It is,' Julia said, with quiet conviction. Someone loved her in the dream, so very much that she lay aching with loss whenever the daylight woke her up. She felt the dream would always vanish when she awoke from it.

The day of Ramona's wedding dawned sunny and warm. Domani was still redolent of the flowers which had been cut from the garden and taken down to the church by Tullio, and for the next couple of hours there was a lot of excited scurrying about as the bride was prepared for the wedding.

In the room where they dressed Ramona the long mirror was wreathed in jasmine, for it was the tradition that a bride should see herself that way on her wedding morning. Her white dress had puffed sleeves, an embroidered bodice and a flounced skirt over several lace petticoats. She wore a gold locket about her neck, and from a little coronet of white flowers there flowed a veil of flowered lace work.

The garment was a traditional Italian one, sent from Sicily by Vitale's grandmother, who was too old and tired to make the journey herself but had desired that her grandson's bride wear the dress and veil which had been in their family for many years. It had been kept in layers of herb-scented linen in a cedarwood chest, and only minor alterations had been needed to make it a perfect fit for Ramona. She looked every inch a true Latin bride, a deep glow of joy and expectancy in her eyes. If she felt saddened that her family had refused to attend the wedding, the feeling was concealed. Not a shadow of doubt about her happiness with Don Vitale showed in her gaze as she turned from the mirror to smile at Julia.

'Do you think Vitale will approve of me?' she asked.

Julia broke into an answering smile. 'He'll love you,' she said simply. 'I've never seen a more charming bride in my life. The dress and veil suit you to perfection, as if they were made for you.'

'You look charming yourself, Julia, and I'm so happy you didn't change your mind about giving me away. I know Rome isn't too happy about it, but you do feel up to it, don't you?'

'I feel fine.' Julia spoke convincingly and kept to herself that upon getting out of bed that morning she had been seized by a dizziness which had flung her to the floor, where she had lain until the room righted itself. If deep inside her she still felt rather odd, she certainly had no intention of telling anyone. She wanted to see Ramona married, and a breath of a hint to Rome that she wasn't as fit as a careful application of make-up made her look, then he'd order her to return home. She couldn't bear the thought of being confined to the villa while everyone else enjoyed this lovely day.

She could feel her spine bracing itself as she walked down to the hall with Ramona, Lucie following with the long veil cradled in her arms. Rome had left for the village an hour ago, so he could lend his support to the bridegroom. He'd had a look of sombre elegance in a dark grey suit, a wine-coloured flower in his lapel. Looking at him when he left in his car, Julia had been irresistibly reminded of her sister's wedding day, when Rome had walked back into her life. It couldn't be denied that he was a remarkably handsome man, except that these days his lean face carried a more serious look.

As they waited in the hall for the wedding car to arrive, Julia could feel Lucie looking at her, concerned that she didn't tire herself. She tilted her chin and smiled, her eyes deep green beneath the dipped brim of a hat in ivory straw, with which she wore a dress of turquoise silk lightly draped about her figure. A crescent of creamy flowers was attached to her dress at the bosom, pinned there by an emerald brooch which Rome had laid casually on the dressing-table when he had asked that morning if she felt strong enough to attend the wedding.

'Don't stop me from going,' she had said.

'I'd stop you, Julia, if I thought it would be better for you.' His eyes had searched her face unsmilingly. 'I don't wish to be a killjoy, but I can't pretend that I wouldn't prefer you to rest at home.'

'I'm not an invalid, Rome.' She gave a laugh, and pushed from her thoughts the dizzy spell which had probably been caused by excitement. 'I haven't done anything to hurt the baby all these weeks, and going to Ramona's wedding won't do him any harm.'

'Him?' A faint smile had touched Rome's lips. 'Is instinct telling you that we're having a son?'

'I wouldn't want that train set to go to waste,' she retorted.

The wedding car drove through the sunlight and into the village, with its crooked streets of houses with flat roofs and walls crusted with limewash, flowers drifting from earthenware pots grouped along sills. Some of the old people stood in their doorways to wave at the car as it passed them, their skin sun-darkened and sculptured into lines from hard work and the gift of laughter.

The car drew to a halt in front of the church, its walls sun-burnished and pierced by coloured windows carved round by fat little *angeli* and cherubs. Stone steps led up to the entrance and two little girls in embroidered dresses helped carry the long lace veil as Ramona entered the coolness of the church to the sound of organ music. Lucie slipped into a seat while Julia continued to walk with the bride to the altar, where Vitale stood in his dark suit beside the taller figure of Rome. Julia felt his encompassing glance as she paused there beside the bride as the music faded and the priest stepped forward to start the ceremony.

At the sound of the Latin words Julia was reminded vividly of her own marriage in New York, where the rows of seats had been empty and the church large and echoing.

When Ramona and Vitale knelt on little red cushions in front of the altar, Julia remembered kneeling beside Rome and feeling his hand warm and hard around hers. She had felt cold and nervous, and so aware that their exchange of vows were not made from love but from expediency. When Rome had bent his tall head to kiss her, she had turned her cold cheek to meet his warm lips ... how warm they had felt, as on that night when pride and passion had swept them together so mercilessly.

Suddenly Julia swayed ... that sickening, spinning feeling was coming over her again. Any second she was going to fall, but before she could do so a strong pair of arms had hold of her and the next instant she was being carried quickly from the church into the sunlight. She heard Rome speak and she heard Lucie answer him. 'Get the doctor!' he said. 'Tell him to come to the villa—*Santo Dio*, her face!

It's so white!'

'Julia?' A hand stroked her cheek. 'Julia, dear one?'

The voice was far away and yet so close . . . so very close. They sped along as through time and space that was made up of shadows and then sudden blinding stabs of whiteness. Tiny claws were tearing at Julia deep inside and she felt bathed in a cold perspiration. She wanted to retch and the car slid to a halt and she was held firmly yet gently so she could give way to her nausea on the roadside.

She was weeping . . . something had gone wrong. It had started to go wrong that morning and she should have told him.

'Rome . . .'

'Hush.' He wiped her forehead. 'Soon we'll be home and I'll put you to bed.'

'I'm so sorry——'

'No sorrier than I am, Julia.'

Her eyelids sank down over her eyes and she lay there, trying not to moan as her body and her heart were clawed by pain. She sensed vaguely that her head was against his shoulder as he drove; she could smell the scent of the flower in his lapel.

'Oh God!'

'Hold on, little one. We're almost home!'

Home . . . on Grand Drive, did he mean? Her head felt so strange, as if it was floating above her shoulders, out into space away from her body that hurt so much.

'Rome——' She slumped and everything went dark.

Through waves of pain and fatigue she came swimming back to a certain awareness. 'I can save your wife or your child, *signore*.' The voice spoke in Italian and she understood every word. 'It is doubtful if I can save both of them, so you must choose.'

Rome made his decision instantly. 'You must save my wife! I can't lose Julia—it would be like losing my own life.'

'Ah, you love her, *signore*.'

'I have loved her since we were children. What caused this to happen to our child?'

'There is no one at fault, not you or your good wife. These things happen, *signore*. All goes well with the pregnancy, then all of a sudden something goes wrong. Nature can be very unpredictable at times.'

'What exactly has happened, *dottore*?'

'The child has breeched and the lower limbs are presenting themselves instead of the shoulders and head. The umbilical cord has twisted around the infant and the oxygen supply is almost cut off. He is being slowly strangled.'

Tears crept down Julia's cheeks and she knew she had to give Rome his son.

'*Dottore*,' she held out a weak hand and spoke in Italian, 'save the baby—my husband wants him so much!'

The doctor leaned over her. 'He wants you even more, *signora*. Nurse, my forceps! *Signore*, perhaps you will hold your wife while we have one final try——'

The words faded and Julia was half lost again in delirium, a warm pair of hands holding her head, a deep voice murmuring her name. Pain wrenched at her and she heard someone curse desperately. 'Don't keep hurting her, for God's sake!'

'The child has to emerge, *signore*, dead or alive!'

Everything was peaceful now. The bedroom lamps diffused a soft, warm glow and the curtains were pulled across the windows. Julia stirred in a soft warm nest and her body felt so curiously slight and young again. Her eyes sought around the room and her heart gave a deep beat as the tall figure turned from the door, where he was speaking to someone, and came swiftly to the bedside. He leaned over her and she lifted a hand to touch his lean, drawn face. Slowly she saw the tears gather and shimmer in his grey eyes.

'I'm so sorry, Rome,' she murmured.

'Sorry?' He allowed a tear to streak his cheek before hastily wiping it away. 'You won't be when you see him, *cara*.'

'Him?'

'Sebastian, our son.' Rome half-turned towards the door. 'Bring him to her, Lucie. Bring the boy.'

'But the doctor said——' Julia couldn't take her eyes from Rome's face. 'I heard him say you had to choose me or the baby. He said the baby was dying——'

'He's a tough one like his father.' Lucie was at the bed-side with a blue-shawled bundle in her arms. She smiled down at Julia. 'Almost blue as this shawl when the doctor pulled him out, but the *signore* took him and breathed into his mouth until he let out such a yell. My, but there's nothing wrong with this *bambino*!'

Julia's eyes were shining as she held out her arms for Rome's son. She felt him, warm and soft, his little rounded cheeks faintly pink. She stroked a finger against the delicate softness of his skin and very slowly he opened his eyes.

Velvety pupils and glimmering grey irises. Rome's eyes, as she had known they would be.

She glanced up eagerly into the eyes she had always loved. That love had gone into hiding for a while ... she hadn't been able to face it that the dark, beautiful boy could grow up a devil who had taken her with such merciless desire that night in Naples.

But now she knew that the desire sometimes had no mercy if the love was overpowering.

Rome leaned down and kissed her, and then very gently the baby. 'Don't leave me,' he whispered. 'I—I couldn't bear it, Julia. I just couldn't face it—I'd have to make you stay, as I made you stay that other time.'

'You don't have to make me, darling,' she whispered back. 'I'm where I want to be, where love is.'

'I've wanted so many times to say it, but each time I advanced you retreated—I could only love you with passion, Julia, never with the refinement you wanted from that other man. I can't help it that I'm Italian.'

Rome's eyes dwelt with a smouldering fire upon her face. 'Have you truly surrendered at last, my one and only love?'

'Oh yes,' she breathed. 'Lucie was right, she said there was no one else——'

'No one that ever mattered—no one at all after that night in Naples, only you. Julia, do you forgive me?'

She glanced at the baby in her arms and slowly smiled. 'You were right, *signore*, we did make this son of ours with passionate love—I know it now. Isn't he just perfect?'

'*Santo Dio*,' Rome groaned, 'a woman is a perfect mystery!'

Lucie smiled and nodded to herself as she slipped quietly from the room and left Julia to bask in the love Rome had always felt for her. The trembling stars hung over Domani—the house of tomorrow.

See over

Just answer these simple questions for your FREE BOOK.

1. **What is the title of the Romance you have just read?**

____

Author's Name ______________________________

2. **Are you a regular Mills & Boon reader?**

Yes ☐ No ☐

(a) If 'No', is this the type of romance you expected?

Yes ☐ No ☐

(b) If 'Yes', is this book up to standard?

Yes ☐ No ☐

3. **Is there any particular type of romance you would like to see from Mills & Boon?**

____

4. **Which age group are you in?**

☐ 16-20, ☐ 21-30, ☐ 31-40, ☐ 41-45, ☐ 45+

5. **What made you buy this book?** (tick one only)

(a) the author ☐
(b) the illustration ☐
(c) the series name ☐
(d) the description of the story ☐
(e) the publisher's name ☐

6. **Are there any comments you wish to make?**

____

____

____

Please post this off today.

Fill in your name and address, put this page in an envelope (you can fold it if you need to) and post today to:-

Mills & Boon Reader Survey, FREEPOST,
P.O. Box 236, Croydon, Surrey. CR9 9EL

NO STAMP NEEDED

Name ______________________________

Address ______________________________

____

______________________________ Postcode ______________

EDQ1